AF269017

MAPLE LEAF MALICE

A COZY QUILTS CLUB MYSTERY

BOOK NINE

MARSHA DEFILIPPO

Copyright © 2026 by Marsha DeFilippo

All rights reserved.

This is a work of fiction. Unless otherwise indicated, all the names, characters, businesses, places, events and incidents in this book are either the product of the author's imagination or used in a fictitious manner. Any resemblance to actual persons, living or dead, or actual events is purely coincidental.

No part of this book may be reproduced in any form or by any electronic or mechanical means, including information storage and retrieval systems, without written permission from the author, except for the use of brief quotations in a book review.

For avoidance of doubt, Marsha DeFilippo reserves the rights, and publishers/platforms have no rights to, reproduce and/or otherwise use the Work in any manner for purposes of training artificial intelligence technologies to generate text, including without limitation, technologies that are capable of generating works in the same style or genre as the Work, unless publisher/platform obtains Marsha DeFilippo's specific and express permission to do so. Nor does publishers/platforms have the right to sublicense others to reproduce and/or otherwise use the Work in any manner for purposes of training artificial intelligence technologies to generate text without Marsha DeFilippo's specific and express permission.

To get the latest information on new releases, excerpts and more, be sure to sign up for Marsha's newsletter.

CHAPTER ONE

"Well, ladies, we made it through February," Eva announced at the weekly Cozy Quilts Club meeting.

"I can't say I'm sad to see it go," Sarah said. "I'm glad it turned out the way it did, though, and Maggie is back home with Ginger."

And not a moment too soon.

Eva heard his comment using her animal whisperer skills and looked down at her cat sitting on the floor beside her chair. "You're not fooling me, Reuben. I could see you were mellowing about Ginger."

Reuben pretended not to hear and stuck out his back leg, grooming it with exaggerated focus—the feline equivalent of a huff.

Eva's friend, investigative reporter Maggie Larkin, had recently been kidnapped to prevent her from testifying at a corruption and bribery trial. The Cozy Quilts Club—Eva, Jennifer, Annalise, and Sarah—had teamed up using their paranormal and computer skills to locate Maggie and ensure her safe rescue. During her captivity, Eva had been taking care of Maggie's dog, Ginger—much to the irritation of her cat, Reuben.

"How are she and Ginger doing?" Jennifer asked.

Eva paused to choose her words. "I think Maggie's still processing what happened, but Ginger is right by her side." Eva chuckled. "Quite literally. I don't think he's left her alone since they got back."

"It'll take time," Annalise said, "but my intuition tells me they're going to be okay."

"Is that your psychic side saying that or regular Annalise?" Sarah asked.

"A little of both," Annalise replied, giving Sarah a wink.

"Changing the subject; when Jim and I went to the Checkout Diner last night, everyone was talking about the Maple Syrup Weekend event at the end of this month. I picked up a flyer, and they're requesting donations for the silent auction," Eva said. Jim Davis was her romantic partner and occasionally partnered with her to solve crimes.

"I didn't know Glen Lake had a maple syrup weekend. What's it about?" Sarah, the only one who didn't live in Glen Lake, asked.

"Oh, it's so much fun. Dave and I and the kids have gone every year. Gregor MacHenry opens his sugar shack to the public for tours so they can see how maple syrup is made. He sells his maple syrup, candy, and fudge. I look forward to buying some every March." Jennifer told her. "Although I'm not sure about the snow taffy. Gregor claims he gets the snow where no one has had access, but..." Jennifer grimaced and shrugged her shoulders.

Sarah's expression softened. "I'd forgotten about snow taffy. We used to make that all the time when I was a kid."

"It was one of the activities that made winter more fun when the kids were growing up. Now that they're eighteen and sixteen, they stick up their noses. 'That's kid stuff.' Then they give me *the look.* The one that's meant to remind me that *you're old, Mom.* "Jennifer smiled and used air quotes as she told the story, eliciting chuckles from the other ladies.

"I'm planning to go this year, too. Liam is making special edition pottery mugs to donate to the auction," Annalise told them. Annalise and Liam had been dating since December when they'd met at the Glen Lake Christmas Craft Fair.

"That's a great segue for me to talk about this month's quilting projects. I was thinking perhaps we could each make one item for the auction using a maple leaf design," Eva said. "I have a pattern for a table runner I've been wanting to make. It's illustrated with fall colors, but I don't think it would be a problem even though it will be springtime when they have the auction. I'd be happy to share it if anyone else is interested."

"Could I use it to make placemats?" Jennifer asked.

"Of course."

"How about my specialty—mug rugs?" Sarah asked.

"You'd have to scale it down quite a bit. The pattern uses ten-inch blocks. You've got the skills to do that, though," Eva replied.

"Or, if you want to go super easy, I'll bet you could find fabric with a maple leaf design at Quilting Essentials," Annalise suggested.

Sarah's face brightened. "That would be amazing! I could make a whole set of them if I didn't have to do much piecing. Thanks!"

"So, we're all on board with our projects?" Eva asked and got thumbs up from the others. "All right. I'll contact the committee in charge of donations and let them know."

"This is just what I needed to get out of my 'why isn't it spring yet?' slump." Annalise said. "It's giving me something fun to look forward to, and by the time it rolls around, the weather should be getting better."

"I hope there won't be any drama about it this year to ruin

the fun," Jennifer began. "Dave and I were at the Diner this week, too. Betty Jones mentioned there's trouble brewing between Gregor MacHenry and his neighbor, Terry Dickinson. Something about a land boundary dispute. Terry decided to start his own maple syrup business, and Gregor claims he's been taking sap from trees on his property."

"Oh, that's not good. Gregor has been known to have a quick temper. Is Terry planning to be part of the Maple Syrup Weekend?" Annalise asked.

"Not if Gregor has anything to say about it," Jennifer replied. "From what Betty said—which I'm taking with a grain of salt considering the source—Deputy Tremblay was called out to break up a fight between them a couple of weeks ago. Gregor claimed Terry was tapping trees on his property. But Terry says they're on *his* property."

"Why don't they have their land surveyed?" Sarah asked. "That would settle it once and for all."

"My guess is neither of them wants to spend the money. Surveys aren't cheap, especially with as much acreage as they each own."

"It could be the snow might still be too deep in the woods," Eva offered.

"That's true. Surveyors can still do it, but it's more challenging. Either way, I hope they settle it soon. I'd hate for the festival to be disrupted by feuding neighbors."

Jennifer paused before adding, "Gregor's poured his whole life into that sugarhouse. He gets… protective. Territorial might be a better word."

A ripple of unease tickled Annalise's intuition. *Feuds often have a way of turning into something worse,* she thought.

"Tell me you didn't just sense something," Sarah said, studying Annalise's face.

"Not really. Nothing specific, anyway. No visions of anything that would need us getting involved."

Sarah nodded but didn't look convinced. From the looks on Eva's and Jennifer's faces, neither were they. And Annalise wasn't entirely sure she was convinced, either.

5

CHAPTER TWO

*H*er playlist was providing background music while Eva hummed along as she looked through her fabric stash for red, orange, and green colors for the table runner project.

Reuben's resting grumpy face was even grumpier this morning. *How long do you plan to have that* music *playing? It's beginning to get on my nerves.*

"Everything gets on your nerves, Reuben. I need my music to keep me pumped up while I'm sewing. I'll be here all week and don't forget to tip your human."

Ugh was Reuben's only response before turning on his heel, much to Eva's amusement.

"Oh, this combination will be perfect," Eva said, not the least embarrassed that she was talking out loud to herself. She checked her pattern for fabric requirements. "No problem, I've got plenty," she said after checking the yardage she had on hand.

Her phone pinged, and she opened the group text from Sarah showing a photo of maple leaf fabric.

Eva replied:

The other ladies echoed her reply.

Not long after, Jennifer sent a group text attaching an image of her fabric choices for the placemats.

Annalise's response was immediately followed up with another message and a photo of Liam's pottery mugs drying on the shelves in his studio.

JENNIFER

How about an assortment of all the fall maple leaf colors?

SARAH

Anything that matches my mug rugs. 

ANNALISE

Haha That would be a perfect complement. I'll pass that along. Maybe we all need a set of both. Get to work, Sarah!

EVA

That's a great idea, Annalise. I'm adding it to my Christmas wish list for Jim.

SARAH

Groan Me and my big mouth.

Three HaHa replies appeared above Sarah's text.

Once Eva finished cutting the pieces for the leaves, she went to her stash again to search for material for the backing, but nothing had just the right blend of colors and patterns.

"Reuben, I'm going to Quilting Essentials. I shouldn't be long. Behave yourself."

Right. Because you so often return home to find me having a party with my feline friends.

"Point taken. How about 'enjoy your nap'?"

That's more like it. Take your time. Wait… is there food in my bowl?

"Unless you've already eaten it. Either way, I seriously doubt you'll starve from malnutrition in the time it takes me to get back. Bye!" Eva didn't wait for his reply.

"HI, Eva. What can I do for you today?" Evelyn Jackson, the owner of Quilting Essentials, greeted her.

"I'm looking for something to use as backing for a table runner." She pulled out swatches of the fabric she'd chosen for the leaves. "I'll be making maple leaves with these and want to coordinate them with the backing."

"We should have just what you need in this section," Evelyn said, leading the way. "Sarah was just in and told me the Quilt Club is making items to donate for the Maple Syrup Weekend."

"That's right."

"The gossip mill is all abuzz. Ginnie Taylor and Irene Nelson were here not long ago and mentioned that Gregor MacHenry and Terry Dickinson are having a feud over their property lines. They said Deputy Tremblay had to go out again to break up another fight." Evelyn was a lifelong Glen Lake resident and, like Betty Jones, heard a lot of the town's happenings through her customers.

"Again? I'd heard he had gone out once, but this was for a new fight?" Eva thought of Annalise's comment the night before about thinking they wouldn't become involved in solving a new crime. A cold shiver ran up her arms—one she couldn't write off as a draft from the shop door.

"Yes. This time Terry claimed his sap buckets had been knocked over. Gregor's side of it was that the trees were his and Terry didn't have permission to be tapping them."

"It sounds like tempers are escalating."

"I agree," Evelyn said. "And those two both have volatile personalities. I just hope they can get it figured out before anyone gets hurt."

"Me, too," a voice behind them said.

Evelyn and Eva turned to see Annalise standing there.

"Annalise, I didn't know you were coming," Eva said.

"Neither did I until I figured out what I want to make and then discovered I was out of double-sided iron-on interfacing."

"We have plenty of that," Evelyn said, smiling.

"I figured you would," Annalise addressed Evelyn, smiling. "Eva, why don't we go to lunch once we're done here? I don't have any clients scheduled this afternoon." Annalise suggested.

"You're on. How about the Diner?"

"You read my mind," Annalise replied.

Eva winked at Annalise's inside joke but couldn't say more with Evelyn standing beside them.

"I think this one would work," Evelyn said, holding up a bolt of Batik fabric with a mottled design that matched the leaf colors perfectly.

"You've done it again, Evelyn. You have a gift for finding just the right colors. I'll take two yards. It's a little more than I need for the project, but I don't mind having scraps left over."

"I'll take it over to the cutting table and have it for you at the checkout counter in just a couple minutes," Evelyn said.

"Would you like to wait until I'm done or just meet at the Diner?" Annalise asked. "I shouldn't be long. The interfacing is all I need today."

"I'll go on ahead and get us a booth."

Twenty minutes later they were sitting at their usual booth with a view of the parking lot when Gregor MacHenry's pickup screeched into a space. He slammed his door shut and stormed inside the diner.

"Oh, my." Annalise was facing the door and followed him with her eyes as he walked to the counter and sat on one of the stools.

"What's going on?" Eva asked, her voice lowered.

"Gregor looks furious. I think something's happened," Annalise whispered.

"Evelyn and I were talking about that just before you came."

Eva recounted the discussion in hushed tones, and when she finished, Annalise stole a look at Gregor. He was hunched over a mug of coffee. In the mirror facing the counter, she could see his scowling face.

"I've got a bad feeling about this," Annalise murmured. She shivered as a flicker of an image flashed behind her eyes—a sap bucket overturned in the snow, the colorless sap pooling in a shallow crater as if someone had ripped it violently from the tree.

"You just saw something, didn't you?" Eva asked.

Annalise described what she'd seen. Eva resisted turning around to look at Gregor.

The words had barely escaped Annalise's lips when Terry Dickinson's truck pulled into the lot. He parked with his truck askew and slammed his door, then stomped into the diner, echoing Gregor's actions of a few moments before.

"You're not going to get away with this," he growled at Gregor, stabbing his finger in the air at him as he spoke.

The diner suddenly fell silent, and Betty Jones hustled over to the men. "You either take this outside or calm yourselves down. I won't tolerate any fights in my diner!" She crossed her arms across her chest and scowled at them.

"I'm leaving," Terry told her. "I'll make sure you pay if you mess with my buckets again," he threatened Gregor and then marched out of the diner. He backed out of his parking space and gravel flew up from his tires as he spun out.

Betty gave Gregor one last warning glance before going back to her duties.

Annalise and Eva exchanged glances, both of them with their eyebrows raised. The other customers resumed their meals; some stealing nervous glances at Gregor.

The rest of their lunch date passed without incident. Gregor left shortly before them, and his departure from the diner was less dramatic than Terry's.

"Guess he finally cooled off," Betty said drily as she watched along with Eva and Annalise as his truck pulled out of the lot.

"We've heard rumors about tempers flaring between them," Eva said.

"The rumors are right." Before she could add more, Betty was called to another booth. She laid their receipts on the table and left.

Eva checked her watch. "I should get home. I'm itching to get sewing now that I have the backing material. I can practically hear my sewing machine calling my name."

"Me, too. We'll talk later."

Eva opened her door to find Reuben staring up at her, his tail flicking in a slow, accusatory rhythm.

I thought you said you wouldn't be long. My bowl is empty. Reuben glared at her with even more attitude than usual.

"Poor baby. However did you survive?" Eva's voice dripped with sarcasm.

Reuben narrowed his eyes even more and haughtily strolled into the kitchen, expecting her to follow.

"Good thing I love that cat," Eva murmured, shaking her head as she followed him like the well-trained human he believed she was.

CHAPTER THREE

Morning light filtered through the windows in Eva's sewing room. The pieces cut for the leaves were neatly arranged like soldiers beside her sewing machine, waiting to be assembled. Her iron was heating up, and the machine was threaded and ready to go. A picture of the block assembly was pinned to the cork bulletin board hung on the wall beside her. Satisfied she had everything she needed, Eva took the first pile and arranged it according to the printout so she could chain stitch them together.

She was in the zone a half hour later when the ping of the phone interrupted her flow. Irritated, she picked up the phone, hoping it wasn't another spam text. Instead, it was a text from Annalise.

ANNALISE

Are you and Jim free tonight? Liam and I are having a date night and thought it would be fun to have you join us.

EVA

I'll check with Jim and get right back to you.

EVA

He's in. What time and where should we meet you?

ANNALISE

Liam suggested O'Malley's at 6. Does that work for you?

EVA

Like a charm. See you later!

Eva went back to her project, but recollection of the incident at the diner popped in unbidden. She tried to shake them off, but the memory triggered a premonitory feeling that it wouldn't be the last altercation between the men.

A persistent rumbling in her stomach finally pulled her out of piecing together both the fabric and reasons for her unease about the fight, and she was surprised to see it was lunchtime.

Looks like a storm's coming. Reuben was staring out the window at the gray sky.

Eva did a double-take. *Is he talking about the weather, or is he feeling something's about to happen, too?* She played it back in her mind, contemplating its possible meanings.

There's not a patch of blue in the sky and the clouds have that gray color to them that usually means they're about to dump snow or rain on us. I'm rooting for rain.

Eva's shoulders relaxed. *You're letting boogeymen get into your head. Stop trying to make more out of something than there is.*

"I'm going to make some lunch. There should be enough chicken left over once I make my sandwich to share some with you, if you're interested."

The cat leaped from the window seat and barreled into the kitchen, nearly tripping Eva up as he flew by.

Eva couldn't help but laugh, lightening her mood. "I take that as a yes."

By four o'clock, Eva had finished the leaf blocks and was ready to call it a day. An added bonus was that her earlier concerns about the diner fight had disappeared and was replaced with excitement about the double-date.

Reuben was curled up on her bed watching Eva. She was muttering under her breath as she slid hangers along the rail, taking an item out, then putting it back before making another selection.

Don't think that one fits anymore.

Too fancy for O'Malley's.

This one's not bad... Is that a stain? When did that happen? And why didn't I use a stain remover when I washed it?

Reuben sat up and finally spoke up, *I assume these are rhetorical questions.*

"What?" Eva looked over at him, her eyes not quite focused, as though surprised to see him there, and then his question registered. "Yes. I was talking to myself."

She resumed her closet search and pulled out a pair of black slacks and a lavender long-sleeved, button-down blouse. "What do you think of these?"

Reuben considered a snarky response, but took pity on her. *I think they'll look quite nice on you.*

Eva stood transfixed, her jaw slightly open, unsure how to respond to the rare compliment. Reuben lay back down and curled his paws together in front of him, then slow-blinked at her, snapping her out of her startled state.

"Why, thank you, Reuben. I'll take your advice on this one."

You must be going out.

"Yes. It's a double-date with Annalise and Liam. Jim's going to pick me up in..." She checked her watch. "Oh, shoot... half an hour. I need to get moving if I'm going to put some makeup on."

She hastily dressed, applied her makeup, and brushed her

hair. The doorbell rang just as she was filling Reuben's bowl for his evening meal.

"Coming!" she shouted, hoping Jim would hear. "I'm leaving. Not sure how long I'll be, but you've got food in your bowl and fresh water," she told him as she walked past the living room.

You kids have fun!

Eva stopped in her tracks and stared at him. *What in the world has gotten into him? He's never this nice.* The doorbell rang again, and she shelved the questions for a later discussion.

"How was your day?" Jim asked once they were on their way.

They spent the rest of the fifteen-minute drive to the restaurant sharing small talk about their respective day's activities. The restaurant was an English pub-style with wooden booths on one side of the room and a long—possibly antique—wooden bar with barstools on the other. Soft Celtic music drifted through the room—lively enough to give the place charm, but at a level that didn't discourage conversation.

Annalise and Liam were already seated and waved to them when they walked in. Liam stood to give Jim a bro hug while Eva slid into the far side of the booth.

Eva inhaled deeply. "What is that heavenly smell?"

"Smells like boiled dinner to me. They're apparently leaning into St. Patrick's Day all month long," Annalise said, referring to the quintessential New England tradition of a corned beef, cabbage, carrots, onions, and potatoes dinner to celebrate the holiday on March seventeenth.

A server arrived at the booth with menus and then announced the specials for the night. They included the boiled dinner and a cheeseburger garnished with maple syrup-cured bacon. She added that the bacon and maple syrup were sourced locally. No one recognized the name of the butcher, but they all knew the maple syrup producer—Gregor MacHenry.

"Now I'm torn between the boiled dinner and the cheese-burger," Eva said after the server left, giving them time to make their selections.

"Why's that?" Jim asked.

"The aroma of that corned beef has my mouth watering, but it would be nice to support our hometown team," she replied.

"Well, if it's just about the bacon, I'll share some from my cheeseburger. Deal?"

Eva smiled. "Deal. I might even give you a bite of the corned beef."

"Speaking of the home team, how are you coming with your table runner?" Annalise asked.

"I got a lot done today. I should have it finished tomorrow or the next day. How about you?"

"Weren't you supposed to remind me not to make such ambi-tious projects the last time I made a landscape quilt?" Annalise teased. "Let's just say I'm glad we've got a month and my Reiki practice isn't fully booked."

"How about you, Liam? Did our suggestions for colors help?"

"They did! I've made an assortment of solids and others with stripes. What I don't donate to the festival, I can sell to the gift shops."

"You might already have a customer for some of those. I've been told my mugs are looking worse for wear," Jim said, giving Eva a side-eye.

Everyone chuckled. They knew he wasn't upset despite the side-eye.

"Happy to save some for you," Liam replied.

"Word around town is that this year is going to be even bigger than last year. Assuming Gregor and Terry don't kill each other before the event." Jim meant it to be in jest, but his smile disappeared when he looked from Annalise to Eva. "What's wrong?" he asked.

"That may be more of a problem than you think it is. Did you know Carl Tremblay has been called out to their properties twice already to break up fights?" Annalise asked.

"And yesterday, we were having lunch at the diner," Eva said, picking up the story from Annalise. "Gregor came in and not long after that Terry pulled up. Terry threatened Gregor that he'd make him pay if Gregor messed with his sap buckets. Betty had to break it up, and Terry peeled out in such a hurry his tires were kicking up gravel."

"I had no idea it had gotten that bad," Jim said. "Some of my buddies in the sheriff's office have mentioned they've had to deal with some run-ins like this. According to them, some people get more territorial about sugar maples than about their own families."

Eva laughed, but Annalise had gone still.

"You okay?" Liam asked. "You look like you've seen a ghost."

Annalise shook her head and smiled. "It's nothing. Just… got a chill."

Annalise was brushing it off, but Eva knew her too well. There was more to this than she was saying, and Eva made a mental note to ask her about it later.

Liam leaned forward, lowering his voice and turning his body slightly to face the others.

"I dropped off a mug order at Pushaw Peddlers this after-noon. Rachel Stevens was watching the shop, and she told me things have escalated between Gregor and Terry again. She lives across the street from them."

"This feels bad. Really bad," Annalise murmured under her breath.

Annalise sat with her hands clenched on the table and rocked back and forth imperceptibly, but Eva caught it. She rubbed her arms as a chill ran up them. Liam and Jim hadn't noticed either woman's reaction, and Liam was continuing his account with Rachel.

"She said Gregor's been out with a metal measuring tape pacing the property line on the street side. And she'd heard voices shouting at each other from the woods. She couldn't make out the words and wasn't a hundred percent sure, but both she and her husband thought it had to be Gregor and Terry."

A brief, sharp pressure built behind Annalise's eyes. She saw a faint image of frosty air and moonlight shimmering off something metallic between tree trunks—and then darkness. Annalise blinked several times and swallowed hard as a wave of nausea washed over her.

Eva had been discreetly watching Annalise and when her knuckles turned white, knew it was time to take a break. "Sorry, hon, but I need to use the ladies' room," she told Jim and slid out of the booth when he moved aside. "Want to come with me?" Eva asked Annalise.

"Yeah, I do."

Annalise rose from the booth, taking a breath that wasn't quite steady. Since her back was to Liam and Jim, only Eva noticed.

Eva checked the stalls once they were in the bathroom to make sure no one else was with them. "You saw something, didn't you?"

"Not clearly. It *could* have been a bucket, but it was more an impression than a detailed image. What went through my head was that something tipped over… and not by accident."

"That's all?" Eva asked.

"As far as the vision goes, but my intuition is telling me this may only be the beginning."

Eva sighed. Annalise was right too often to dismiss it.

"We should probably get back," Annalise said to break the silence.

Their meals had arrived when they returned, and conversation moved on from the maple syrup rivalry. It was only early March, and the air was still crisp, especially at night. The foursome walked to their cars together, their breath floating in the air visible in the light from the streetlamp. Snow crunched under their boots, and in the distance, an owl hooted. Instinctively, Liam reached for Annalise's hand, and Jim put his arm around Eva's shoulders for protection. The couples said their goodbyes and drove into the night.

"This was fun. We should do it more often," Jim said after they'd driven a few miles in silence.

Eva had been looking out the side window, but turned to Jim. "Hmmm?"

He repeated his words, and this time they got through. She smiled at him in the dim light of the car. "That's a good idea."

She caught Jim's questioning look and rambled on about potlucks and round-robin dinners to keep him from asking more pointed questions. He'd been a police officer and was observant. Had there been more light for him to see her features, it might not have worked.

Once they arrived at her house, Eva begged off having him come in for a nightcap. She wasn't up for it. Her conversation in the bathroom with Annalise echoed in her thoughts.

Reuben barely stirred when she walked over, but slit his eyes and stretched his body out when she stroked his fur.

"Something's wrong, Reuben. I don't know what… but something's wrong."

Reuben licked his paw, paused, and looked at her.

Humans always think they have time to make things right. They rarely do.

Eva felt a jolt run through her and shivered. His words struck a chord, and the seed that something was wrong planted itself in her gut. She dressed for bed. She hoped her sleep would be dreamless, but she knew it wouldn't come easily.

CHAPTER FOUR

Several tables were occupied by the morning regulars at the Checkout Diner, sipping coffee and exchanging banter and laughter with the occupants of their neighboring tables. Glen Lake was no exception to the classic small-town trope—everyone knew everyone, and no story stayed secret for long.

"There's Jim," Liam told Annalise, whose back was to the door. Liam waved to catch Jim's attention, and he walked over to their booth.

"We have to stop meeting like this. Eva's going to get suspicious," Jim teased.

"Come join us, anyway," Liam said, standing to make room for Annalise, so Jim could take her spot on the opposite bench seat.

"Don't mind if I do. Eva should be along any minute. I have some errands to do, so we drove in our own cars."

"Speak of the devil," Annalise said before calling Eva's name. When Eva turned and saw them, Annalise took her spot next to Liam.

"It's déjà vu all over again," Eva joked.

Betty came to the booth with two mugs and a carafe of coffee. She filled the cups without asking and refilled Liam and Annalise's. "Do you need a menu, or do you already know what you want?"

"No need for me," Jim told her and gave his order. The others followed suit. As regular customers at the diner, they knew the menu's breakfast choices by heart.

"Liam and I were saying we should do more double-dates. We had a great time," Annalise said.

"We were talking about that on the way home, too. I was thinking we might even start doing more potluck dinners, but include our partners. We could make it a round robin so no one couple would have to be the host," Eva suggested.

Liam looked to Annalise before replying. "I like that idea, but I can't speak for Annalise."

"It works for me, too." Annalise remembered how nervous she'd been making Liam part of their group when they first started dating. She realized now that she had nothing to worry about. He'd blended in as if he'd always been one of them.

"Then it's agreed. We can bring it up at the meeting tonight so Jennifer and Sarah can weigh in," Eva said.

"Did you hear the neighbors had to call the cops again this morning? Gregor and Terry were at it again," Betty said as she placed their meals on the table. "After their dust-up here yesterday, I'm not too surprised."

"Do you know what they were fighting about?" Jim asked.

"Terry claimed Gregor had dumped some of his buckets off the trees in the night. Then it was the usual 'they're not your trees, they're mine' from Gregor and the hollering began. Rachel Stevens was the one who called the cops."

Annalise and Eva exchanged glances. They both were thinking the same thing—that had to be what her vision was about the night before. It fit the image she'd seen of moonlight shining on something metallic.

"Deputy Tremblay is the officer they sent out from the sheriff's office. I think he's losing his patience with both of them," Betty continued.

"That's saying a lot. Carl's known for being level-headed and able to defuse volatile situations like this," Jim said.

"That's true. I can't say that I blame him, though. This is getting to be a daily thing with those two," Betty replied.

"I don't remember hearing anything about them having trouble before this year," Annalise chimed in, "and I've lived in Glen Lake nearly all my life."

"It's the maple syrup thing. I think Terry figured if Gregor could make money at it, he could, too. Their maple groves are right next to each other," Betty said.

She paused and scanned the room as though taking attendance of who was still within earshot. Once she was satisfied the subject of her next comment wasn't there, she continued, but still lowered her voice as insurance.

"Gregor hasn't had any competition, and he's gotten used to being the top dog. It might not have been a problem if Terry didn't build his own sugar shack and ask to be part of the Maple Syrup Weekend."

"I'm new here, but why didn't the festival committee limit it to one type of business and alternate years they could enter?" Liam asked.

"Last year there were complaints that Gregor's place was so crowded, some people couldn't get in during the times when he had the tours. My guess is they thought with another vendor, it would solve that problem," Annalise told him.

"I doubt they had any idea it would cause this much trouble. I spoke to Olivia Perry... she's the chairperson for the festival committee," Eva explained for Jim's benefit, "last week about the Quilts Club donations for the silent auction. She seemed beside herself because of it. In fact, she's the one who brought it up. I think she needed to vent to someone."

"Well, that's life in a small town. There's always some drama for people to talk about. I've got another customer flagging me down. Enjoy your breakfast," Betty said, and bustled off.

"And she's also the one who talks about it the most," Annalise whispered and leaned forward, so Betty wouldn't hear.

"I have some errands to run, so I should get moving," Jim said, pulling out his wallet. He reached for Eva's tab, checked the amount, and handed her a twenty-dollar bill along with the tab for his breakfast. "This should cover them and the tip. I'll call you later."

"Why, thank you," Eva told him, her cheeks turning a pale pink when he leaned down to kiss her cheek before walking into the convenience store side of the building.

"I should go, too. I have a client coming in an hour," Annalise said.

Liam took their checks before standing to leave with her. "Can't let Jim show me up," he told Annalise when she held out her hand for hers.

"All right, but next time it's my treat. I'll see you tonight, Eva."

"You bet. I should have the runner done for show and tell if I stop dawdling here."

At the convenience store, Jim was checking his shopping list to make sure he'd put everything he needed into his basket when Terry Dickinson approached him. Jim sighed silently when he noticed Terry's awkward posture. Jim had seen that look before during his time as a state trooper and it sent up a red flag that he was about to be put on the spot.

"Hey, Jim."

"Hello, Terry. How are you doing today?"

"Not bad. Could be better," he paused as though working up the courage to ask what he really wanted from Jim. "You were a cop before you retired, right?"

"State trooper," Jim replied.

"Well… what advice would you give someone who was having trouble with their… neighbor… crossing a line? Hypothetically, of course."

"Depending on what the trouble was, I might tell them to try to work it out between themselves."

"And if they couldn't?" Terry asked.

"Is this about your trouble with Gregor?" Jim asked pointedly.

"You've heard about that?"

"I think everyone in town has heard about it," Jim replied. "When people can't work things out between themselves, they have options. But I'm not a lawyer. Your best bet would be to contact yours, if you have one. Or get one if you don't."

"Yeah… yeah… I suppose that's the best way to handle it." Terry scuffed his shoe on the wooden floor, as though embarrassed. "Lawyers are expensive, though. I was hoping there might be something else I could do."

"Not getting one could be even more expensive if things escalate," Jim advised.

Terry considered Jim's words for a moment, then nodded his head. "Thanks, Jim. Appreciate the advice."

"I hope you'll get your problem settled amicably," Jim told him.

"Me, too."

Jim watched Terry walk away. His shoulders were slumped as he trudged slowly to the front of the store. *Looks like he's carrying the weight of the world on his shoulders,* Jim thought.

Terry paused just before pushing the door open and looked down at the display of maple syrup and candy—Gregor MacHenry's—and then shoved the door open with more force than was necessary, making it rattle in its frame. Jim followed with his eyes as Terry pulled out of the parking lot and then returned to his shopping, their conversation soon forgotten.

CHAPTER FIVE

Gregor MacHenry put on his winter jacket and wool gloves, stepped into his Bean boots, and strode out of his house like a soldier preparing for battle. This was going to be the day he caught Terry Dickinson in the act of tapping his trees. He felt it in his bones. *And when he did*—this would be the last day Terry would ever steal sap from his maples.

The sun shone brightly, reflecting off the white snow so much, that he had to squint against the glare. The path to the maple grove had packed the snow down into a solid two-inch base, dulling some of the crunching noise of his steps, but he walked slowly to hide his approach as much as possible. He didn't want Terry to hear and sneak back to his house like the thief he was.

The woods were unusually quiet and a sense of unease simmered in his belly, but he shrugged it off. As he walked, though, even the drip of sap into buckets seemed muted, as though the forest itself were on edge. An omen of something bad about to happen.

Gregor had nearly reached the contested trees when he

stopped in his tracks. He shaded his eyes to focus on the object lying in the path ahead of him.

Is that...? He took a few more steps, and the shape took form in his brain. It was a man—and he was hurt. All thoughts of defending his property against Terry Dickinson flew from his mind, and then he ran.

"Terry. Terry, are you all right?" He knelt by Terry's side and gently shook his shoulder. Terry was lying prone with his head turned to the side, his eyes closed, but he didn't respond to Gregor's touch.

Gregor leaned his ear close to Terry's mouth, then removed his gloves and placed two fingers under Terry's collar to check for his pulse. It was faint, but still there. For a split second, an ugly thought surfaced—*maybe this is his punishment for stealing my sap.*

The shame followed immediately. Whatever Terry had done, he didn't deserve this. *It was just sap.* Right now, this was a man who needed help. And in this town, neighbors helped neighbors when it came to situations like this.

He scanned his eyes over Terry's body, and it didn't look like he had any broken bones.

Just as he was about to turn him over, the caution about not moving anyone because it could cause more injury—maybe even paralyze them, stopped him. Terry was still breathing, so he didn't need CPR—it should be all right to leave him as he was.

"Hold on Terry, I'm going to get help."

Gregor reached into his pocket for his phone but found it empty. He swore softly. He didn't want to leave Terry, but he had to call 911 and to do that he had to go back to his house.

Terry moaned and Gregor leaned down close to his face to hear him. Only garbled words came out.

"I can't understand you. Say that again."

Gregor waited, but there was nothing more. He sat up and realized Terry was unconscious again.

"I'm going to have to leave you, Terry. I don't have my phone with me and I need to call 911, but I'll be right back."

Gregor took off his coat and laid it across Terry to keep him warm. His heart raced as adrenaline pushed him to run as fast as he could back to his house. He'd forgotten to put his gloves back on, and his fingers were stiff from the cold as he fumbled with the door. The seconds felt like minutes before the door flung open and he ran into the house, not bothering to close the door behind him.

He yanked the charging cord out of the phone and stabbed the numbers 911. *"Come on… come on…"* he muttered to the silence on the line until finally he heard a ring, and a voice announced: "911. What is your emergency?"

"I need an ambulance. I just found my neighbor in the woods and he needs help."

JIM SLOWED down when he saw the flashing lights of a sheriff's vehicle and an ambulance pulled to the side of the road ahead of him. Curiosity turned to concern when he recognized where they were—Gregor MacHenry and Terry Dickinson's property.

He pulled onto the shoulder and checked for passing traffic before exiting his vehicle. A sheriff's deputy was emerging from the woods and looked up, meeting Jim's eyes.

"Looks like things finally got physical," Jim said, nodding his head toward the ambulance.

"Not exactly. Gregor says he found Terry unconscious in the maple grove. He called 911 but Terry was dead by the time the EMTs got here." His eyes leveled with Jim's. "You didn't hear that from me. We still need to do the notification."

"Of course. Cause of death?" Jim asked.

"Looks like it's natural causes. The medical examiner is on

the way and they'll do an autopsy, but that's the preliminary finding."

Another car pulled up behind Jim's and a man stepped out carrying a CSI kit bag.

"The ME's here. I'll get out of your way."

Jim walked back to his car. "Mornin', Ian." He said as he passed the medical examiner, Ian Nelson. They'd worked together many times before.

"Mornin, Jim. What brought you here?"

"Neighborly curiosity. I'm leaving now if you want to pull your car up."

"Might just do that," he said, but continued walking and followed Deputy Tremblay into the woods.

Jim's mind returned to his conversation with Terry as he drove the rest of the way home. He hoped it would turn out to be natural causes, but what if it wasn't? Things didn't always turn out that way.

All I did was advise him to get a lawyer. What if I should have told him to ask for more protection? A restraining order…? Jim stopped that line of thinking. Even restraining orders weren't always enough.

Rationally, he knew it was his cop training kicking in, but it hadn't escaped him that he'd had the thought that Gregor could be responsible.

Carl said it was natural causes. Leave it at that.

Jim switched the station on his radio to a talk show and forced himself to focus on the discussion to divert his attention. His hands tightened on the steering wheel, but despite the noise of the hosts of the talk show yammering away, the thought nagged at him that he should have done more.

CHAPTER SIX

*E*va rolled her shoulders and leaned her head from side to side to work out the kinks in her neck. She'd been sewing all morning and needed a break for lunch. She turned on the under-counter TV to catch the weather forecast while she made her sandwich. Her hand froze in mid-air when she heard the top of the hour news report. Eva's hand trembled as she set the knife on her plate—her sandwich preparation would wait.

A man was found unresponsive near a private sugarhouse off the Old Maple Road in Glen Lake. He was pronounced dead at the scene. Early indications are the death was from natural causes, but an autopsy will be performed to determine the cause of death. The name of the victim is being withheld pending notification of next of kin.

THERE WERE two sugarhouses at that location—Gregor's and Terry's.

"Oh, no. Which one of them?"

The shock of hearing either Gregor or Terry was dead shut down the hunger that had driven her to the kitchen. Eva wrapped her arms around herself, the room suddenly cold. She had to talk to someone and ran through the list of names, settling on Jim's.

"Jim can get information I can't," she reasoned.

About what? Reuben asked. *Not that I care, but you look like you need to vent to someone.*

"Not now, Reuben. Someone has died and I don't need your snark."

The tip of his tail twitched as he turned to leave the room.

Eva hated that she'd snapped at him. Yes, his comment had been rude, but it wasn't as though he had any emotional attachment to a random—for him—person dying. Despite the sarcasm, he'd been offering his version of solace to her.

"Sorry, I shouldn't have taken it out on you," Eva called after him, but the damage was already done and she knew it would be awhile before he spoke to her again.

"Jim, I just heard the news," she began when he answered her call. "They're saying a man died. It's got to be Gregor or Terry from the location they gave. Have you heard anything about it?"

She sensed his hesitation. That couldn't be good.

"I'm not supposed to say anything, but I was passing by when the first responders were there. I talked to Carl Tremblay, and he told me it's Terry. Gregor found him and called 911, but they couldn't save him. You can't tell that to anyone, though."

"Not even the club? You know they won't spread it around if I say it's confidential."

Eva waited for Jim's response. *I shouldn't have put him on the spot like that,* she chided herself.

"As long as you make it very clear that until an official announcement is made, they have to keep it to themselves. I trust them, but I have to say that, anyway."

"I promise. Thank you, Jim. I'm going to call Annalise.

Knowing her, she's probably already had a vision. I'll see you later. You're still coming over for dinner, aren't you?"

"You bet. Maybe by then we'll know more."

They disconnected and Eva called Annalise, hoping she wasn't in a Reiki session so she could talk.

"Have you heard the news?" Eva asked.

"I've had clients all morning, but I've had a feeling something was wrong trying to surface. I had to keep it suppressed while I was working, though. What's happened?"

"Jim told me this in confidence." Eva recounted their discussion. "I promised him you wouldn't say anything after I told you."

"Of course. This is terrible." Annalise hesitated, weighing her words. "I know they've said natural causes but I don't think either one of us believes that."

"Actually, I think I was hoping you would tell me it was."

CHAPTER SEVEN

By the time the Quilts Club met the next evening, the news had spread in Glen Lake and it was no longer a secret Terry Dickinson was the man who'd been found dead. Only Sarah hadn't heard, but Eva thought it safe to share the information.

The room had a more subdued energy. It was as though everyone was waiting for the other shoe to drop. The one that meant they would become involved, if for no other reason than that was what had happened every month for the nearly nine months they'd been together.

"They announced it on the early evening news," Jennifer said. "They're still saying Terry died from natural causes pending autopsy."

"I hope it was. Considering the fighting between him and Gregor, it could have been something worse," Sarah said.

"That's not what happened," Annalise stated with certainty. "I don't know *what* happened yet, but it wasn't natural causes and it wasn't an accident."

The room grew quiet. The other shoe had dropped.

Eva cleared her throat and broke the silence. "Jim happened

to be going by not long after they found him, and Deputy Tremblay gave him some of the details. This is for your ears only. Jim told me in confidence, but said it would be okay to tell you because he could trust you to keep it to yourselves." The ladies nodded their consent before Eva continued.

"Gregor found Terry lying in the snow on the path to his—Terry's," she added for clarification, "house and called 911. He was alive then, but by the time the EMTs got there, it was too late. He was gone. They don't have any reason to think it's suspicious, so the autopsy is a formality. At least for now." A look passed between her and Annalise; one that said, 'I believe you that it's more than that.'

"After you called yesterday to give me the news, I still couldn't shake the feeling something bad had happened. I had the feeling there was more to it, and I kept waiting for clarity. It never came—and that bothers me more. It's as if there's a shadow—or a presence—blocking me."

"Are they still going forward with the Maple Syrup Weekend?" Sarah asked.

"I haven't heard otherwise. It will be like all the past years with just Gregor handling the tours so they might have to recalibrate that part of the festival. They'd hoped to handle the overload with Terry's sugarhouse," Eva said.

"There's a rumor going around that Terry's brother, Donald, is going to step in for him. He wanted to do it in Terry's memory," Jennifer said.

"I hope Gregor won't have a problem with that."

"Me, too, Eva. Even if Terry was tapping the trees on Gregor's property, I honestly don't think it was malicious. I think he truly believed the trees were on his land."

"Having the land surveyed will be even more of an issue now. Who inherits Terry's property?" Sarah asked.

Eva, Annalise, and Jennifer looked to each other for the answer, but none of them knew.

"Terry wasn't married and didn't have any children. If he didn't have a Will, I guess it would pass to Donald because their parents are already deceased." Jennifer was the first to reply. "He's Terry's only living sibling."

"I heard Gregor wanted to buy the land years ago, but Terry's dad refused his offer. He thought it should stay in the family and Terry was the oldest. They've owned it for several generations and that's how it's always been passed down. The oldest male child inherited it," Annalise added.

Eva thought the conversation about Terry had run its course and wanted to lighten the heaviness that hung in the air.

"Why don't we move on to why we're here? Keeping our hands busy might help. Who wants to go first for show and tell?"

CHAPTER EIGHT

"I have to run up to the Checkout, Reuben. I ran out of half and half."

Unless you're getting me a can of tuna while you're there, I really don't need to know. Reuben's icy mood had thawed since Eva had snapped at him, but not completely.

At least he's speaking to me again, Eva thought. "I'll see what they've got. I should be back in a few minutes."

Eva noted it was busier than usual for the time of day on a weekday as she slipped into the last open parking space. A doorbell chimed a single ding-dong when she entered the store.

"Hi, Eva. It's beginning to feel like spring out there," Jerry Hopkins, one of the store's clerks, greeted her.

"Don't let it fool you. There's still the chance of more snow before winter's officially over."

"Yeah. It's probably wishful thinking on my part," Jerry replied sounding discouraged, and Eva instantly regretted her choice of words.

"Sorry, didn't mean to burst your bubble. And you're absolutely right. It won't be long before we have even more of these nice days."

Jerry's young face brightened.

Eva took one of the wire baskets to carry her purchases. She'd thought of a couple other things she needed on the drive to the store. After getting the half and half, she went to the aisle with canned tuna. She already had a can at home, but thought showing Reuben she'd listened to his request was a good idea.

Two women she didn't know were talking in the next aisle over and Eva heard Terry's name. She didn't mean to eavesdrop, but voices carried in a small store like the Checkout.

"I wouldn't be surprised if Gregor MacHenry is responsible for Terry's death," one of them said.

"Me, either. He's always had a bad temper and everyone knew they hated each other."

"Have you heard why he died?"

"No. Terry did have a bad heart, so I suppose it *could* have been a heart attack," the second woman said, but her tone didn't match her sentiment.

"Until the autopsy report confirms that, my money's on Gregor snapping. It might not have been planned, but either way, Terry's still dead."

Eva had been pretending to scan the shelves as they talked but moved on to finish her shopping once they'd walked away.

Gloria Banks was ahead of her in the checkout line and turned when she recognized Eva.

"I thought that was you," she said.

Eva's heart skipped a beat thinking she'd been caught listening, but relaxed when she realized Gloria hadn't been one of the women gossipers.

"Hello, Gloria. How are you today?"

"I'm doing just fine. And it's so good to have Maggie and Ginger back at home." Gloria lived across the street from Maggie Larkin. That Gloria was a busybody had been a plus for a change. She'd given them a partial license plate number that had helped identify Maggie's kidnappers.

"I couldn't agree with you more."

Jerry was almost finished ringing up Gloria's purchases and Eva thought their conversation was over, but Gloria asked, "Will I see you at the Maple Syrup Weekend?"

"I'll be there along with the other ladies in our quilt club. We're making items to donate for the silent auction and Jim and I always get a bottle or two of maple syrup. You can't beat locally made syrup."

"It's such a shame about Terry, but I heard his brother, Donald, is going to fill in for him."

"I heard that, too. I don't know if that's been decided for sure, though."

Gloria looked around to see if anyone was close enough to hear, then leaned in toward Eva and whispered, "I'm surprised they didn't tell Gregor he was out of the festival."

Eva made a mental note that Gloria hadn't lowered her voice enough that Jerry wouldn't be able to hear, apparently unconcerned if he did.

"Why would they do that?" Eva asked, speaking at a normal level.

"Well, you know. Out of respect for Terry. I mean, after all the brouhaha between him and Gregor over the last couple of weeks, and now Terry's dead." She emphasized "dead," and raised her eyebrows as though to put an exclamation point on her statement.

The doorbell sounded as the door opened and Gregor MacHenry walked in. Eva noted the way he slouched and the circles under his eyes, as though he hadn't been sleeping well.

As soon as Gloria spotted Gregor, she handed Jerry the cash for her purchases and took her grocery bags. "I'll see you later, Eva."

She brushed past Gregor without acknowledging him and Eva noticed Gregor's hurt expression. The women who had been gossiping about him earlier had been on their way to the checkout lane, but turned in unison to avoid being near him. Their behavior hadn't been subtle even to Gregor, and he scowled at their retreating backs and stuffed his hands in his coat pockets.

"Hello, Gregor," Jerry greeted him, drawing his attention away from the women.

Gregor's face brightened a little. "Hello, Jerry." Eva felt a pang of sadness at how gratefully Gregor responded to the small kindness. It was like he was thinking *At least not everybody suspects me.*

"Nice to see you, Gregor," she said.

"You, too, Eva. You sure you should be talking to me?" He said it in a joking way, but Eva knew he meant it seriously. "Seems like most people are clamming up when they see me lately."

"Jim told me you were the one who called 911 and tried to get help for Terry," she said raising her voice a little so the women could hear.

"Yeah. I'm a real hero," he replied, his sarcasm obvious. "I know a lot of people have been whispering behind my back. Terry and I had our disagreements, but that was business. It wasn't something to kill anyone over."

Eva glanced over at the women, who by now were loitering in the aisle farthest away from the door. Both of their faces flushed a dark shade of pink, but they kept their eyes lowered.

She hadn't planned to get involved but small-town gossip could ruin a person's reputation permanently. Until there was more proof—official proof—of his guilt, Eva was willing to keep an open mind.

"You hang in there, Gregor. I should get home. I have a cat that thinks he's on the brink of starvation despite having already been fed today."

"See you, Eva. And thanks."

She gave him a warm smile and left. It wasn't until she was

in the car and turned on the ignition that it hit her. She replayed her thought—*until the police had more proof.* Had it been a Freudian slip?

She wanted to keep an open mind. But the drive home was consumed with thoughts of the possibility—or probability—that Gregor could have killed Terry. She didn't want to believe it, but if Terry had been murdered, who other than Gregor had a motive?

Reuben was waiting in the kitchen for her and twined himself through her legs when she took the can of tuna out of the bag. Eva even thought she heard a soft purr. Reuben sensed her distraction and stopped.

What's got you so worried?

For once there was genuine concern without any of Reuben's usual snark.

"I ran into Gregor MacHenry at the store," Eva said. "Seems like everyone's already decided he's guilty of murdering Terry Dickinson."

Reuben's tail flicked once. "And you?"

Eva opened the can of tuna, buying herself a moment. "I'm hoping he's not the quilt club's next case."

CHAPTER NINE

"Apart of me wanted to march over and tell those women what for," Eva said, stabbing her fork in the air.

Jim had listened quietly while she'd recapped her visit to the convenience store that afternoon.

"I felt so sorry for Gregor. I could see how humiliated he was, and he looks like he's aged ten years."

"This has to be hard on him. Having friends and neighbors you thought would have your back treat you like that is a punch in the gut," Jim said. "I'm not sure it's something you can ever fully get over even if you're vindicated."

"You don't think he's guilty, do you?" Eva asked.

"I had too many years on the force to jump to any conclusions until all the facts are in."

"Speaking of which, have you heard anything about the autopsy results?"

"Nothing official. One of my buddies said it wasn't as straightforward as they'd thought at the scene, so it's taking longer."

"What do you think that means?" Eva asked, her curiosity piqued.

"It could mean a lot of things. But if I had to guess? They ruled out a heart attack."

"Or natural causes?" Eva asked.

Jim smiled. "You don't really think you can trick me into saying more than this, do you?"

Eva shrugged. "Can't blame a girl for trying."

Girl? Really? That went out the window fifty years ago, Reuben sniffed.

"It's just an expression, Reuben." Eva pretended to be indignant, but was secretly pleased to hear the snark. It meant he'd forgiven her and was ready to get back to life as usual at Casa Perkins.

"Should I ask?" Jim knew about their spat and had watched the exchange with amusement.

"It's just Reuben being Reuben."

Reuben gave her a slow blink and went back to his perch in the living room.

"Now that he's gone, does that mean he's talking to you again?"

"Yes." Eva smiled. "I knew he'd come around, but it's nice to have it behind us sooner than later."

JIM CALLED the next morning to give her an update.

"I wanted to let you know before you heard it on the news. Carl told me the autopsy results are in and Terry's death wasn't from natural causes. They're considering it a homicide."

"Do they think Gregor did it?"

Jim didn't answer her question directly. "I'd thought you'd be more surprised to hear the homicide angle," he said instead. "You sound like that's what you were expecting all along."

"Annalise has had hints that it wasn't how Terry died," Eva said. That told Jim all he needed to know.

"Does she think it's Gregor?" he asked.

"She doesn't know who it is. She hasn't been getting visions in the usual way. They're more just impressions that there's more going on under the surface."

Jim sighed, the sound heavy with resignation. "I suppose this means the quilts club will be getting involved."

"I don't know… Probably." She paused to gather her thoughts. "It seems like we've been brought together for this reason by forces outside ourselves. It's not something we ever planned."

"I didn't mean it to come out as an accusation. If it did, I'm sorry."

"I know. I assume it's okay to tell the ladies about this since it will be on the news?"

"It should be. I can't think of any reason why not and it's probably already making the rounds on the grapevine, anyway."

"Thanks, Jim. I really do appreciate that you told me."

"You bet. We'll talk later."

Eva tapped Annalise's number, expecting voice mail, but Annalise answered.

"Jim just called to let me know the autopsy results concluded Terry's death is a homicide."

Annalise felt a light clenching of her stomach muscles and a sense of resignation at the news. "That just confirms what I've suspected. If I'd been wrong, the feeling would have gone away, but it hasn't. I can still only see a shadow, so I can't rule Gregor out—or in—as the killer."

"Jim asked if we're going to be getting involved." Eva phrased it as a statement, but Annalise knew it was also a question.

"I don't see how we have any choice about it," Annalise said, echoing Eva's sentiments.

"That's what I was afraid you'd say."

CHAPTER TEN

"Is it okay if we sit with you?" Eva asked Jennifer when she and Jim arrived at the church for Terry's funeral two days later.

"Of course. I was just about to go inside to save us a seat. David dropped me off to park the car. I think the entire town showed up," Jennifer replied looking around at the swarm of people heading into the building.

"Jim and I came together and had the same problem," Eva told her. "I wish we'd thought to have you drop me off first."

"We should probably go in now or none of us will have a seat," Jim suggested quickly when he saw the look Eva was giving him. She'd complained about walking in heels all the way from the car to the church.

Had they waited any longer, they would have been out of luck. David arrived minutes later, out of breath.

"The church lot was full, so I had to park on the side of the road. It's a good thing I don't have a problem parallel parking. The spot I found was a little tight, but I got the car in," he whispered to Jennifer, then leaned across her to say hello to Jim and Eva.

Terry's brother, Donald, looking pale and nervous, gave the eulogy. His words faltered at first but as he told stories about growing up with Terry that had the attendees laughing, his confidence grew.

When the minister asked if anyone else would like to say a few words, several people, including David, took the opportunity to share their memories.

"There will be a reception in the church basement following the internment, but you are welcome to remain here if you prefer not to attend," Reverend Carlson announced.

"I'm okay with staying for the reception, but I'd rather not try to find another place to park the car unless you really want to go to the internment," David said to Jennifer. The town's cemetery was a mile from the church.

"I don't need to go," Jennifer said and turned to Eva and Jim. "We're going to go to the basement now so David doesn't have to move the car."

"I like that idea, too," Jim said.

"That's fine with me," Eva replied.

They joined the others milling around in the basement. It was still set up with banquet tables covered in white linens and folding chairs from the baked bean supper held there a few days before. Church volunteers had prepared assorted finger sandwiches and desserts which they were setting out for the attendees. On a separate table, beverages—hot and cold—were available. A few bouquets from those sent for the funeral had been brought downstairs and placed on the table with the refreshments.

Eva noticed Gregor MacHenry standing awkwardly by himself at the rear of the room.

"I'm going to invite Gregor to come sit with us unless anyone would rather I didn't," Eva said, standing.

The others looked over at Gregor and then back at Eva before telling her they didn't mind.

"I'll go with you," Jim offered. "Just in case you have to run the gauntlet," he teased.

Gregor drew back slightly when he saw Eva and Jim approach.

"Would you like to join us? We're with Jennifer and David Ryder and there's plenty of room for you there," Eva said, smiling.

"No reason for you to stand here by yourself when you have friends to be with," Jim said, clapping Gregor on the shoulder.

"Thank you. I'd be happy to join you," Gregor said, gratefully.

Eva and Jim walked on either side of him, ignoring the furtive glances and whispers behind hands as they walked to join the Ryders. Some even turned their backs to them when they passed. David rose to shake Gregor's hand and offered him the seat beside him.

"I almost didn't come," Gregor began. "But I wanted to pay my respects even though I knew some people in town might not like it."

"Not everyone feels that way," Jennifer said, meeting Gregor's eyes.

"I suppose that's true. You don't," he said offering a weak smile. "But since they announced the autopsy reports, even more people are treating me like I'm a suspect."

"Have the police questioned you?" Jim asked.

"A couple detectives came to my house. Do you know them, Jim? Said their names were Robertson and Smith."

The other four all smiled. "Turns out we all know them," Jim replied.

"They're good men and good detectives," Eva said. "They'll be fair with you and you can trust them."

"I get how Jim might know them but how do the rest of you?" Gregor asked.

"Let's just say our paths have crossed a time or two," Jennifer told him, but declined offering any additional details.

"I'll get you something to eat if you're hungry," Jim offered to Eva.

"Since you're offering," she said, smiling. "I'll have egg salad or tuna and a couple cookies. And maybe some chips. And some of those little gherkins if they have some."

"You've got it. How about you, Gregor? I don't mind."

Gregor was aware why Jim offered and gladly accepted.

"I'll have the same, but make it two sandwiches. Those things are tiny."

"I'll come with you," David offered and accompanied Jim once Jennifer had told him her choices.

They shared small talk while they ate and Eva noticed Gregor had finally relaxed.

The conversations in the room hushed when Donald and Reverend Carlson entered. The reverend whispered in Donald's ear before picking up a glass and lightly tapping on it with a spoon to get everyone's attention. The room stilled.

Donald cleared his throat, his discomfort back when he saw everyone's eyes were on him.

"I'd just like to say thank you to everyone for coming. I know Terry would have been humbled by your support—and so am I." He shifted nervously.

"Um. Thanks. I guess that's all," he concluded awkwardly.

The reverend stepped in. "And thank you to the volunteers who put together this reception. I think Terry would be pleased."

"He always did like a free meal," Donald said, joking. The room erupted with laughter, breaking the somber mood that had hung over it and resumed their conversations.

Jennifer looked up just as Donald glanced in their direction. His jaw set and his eyes hardened when he spotted Gregor. For a moment, she was afraid he would make a scene, but Gloria

Banks saved them when she put her hand on Donald's arm to offer her condolences.

She wasn't the only one who'd noticed. Gregor was staring back at Donald.

"I think it's time for me to go," Gregor said. "Thanks for the food and the company."

He nodded a goodbye and took his empty paper plate and cup, dumping them in the trash can and left without speaking to anyone on his way out the door.

A chill ran up Jennifer's spine when she looked again at Donald. Gloria was still babbling away but Donald's eyes were fixed on Gregor's retreating figure.

Something is wrong about this. It's more than grief—or even anger. And more than what happened between Terry and Gregor. Something isn't adding up. Jennifer couldn't put her finger on it, but a sense of unease came over her.

A half hour later, Jim and Eva announced they were ready to leave.

"We should go, too. I want to say goodbye to Donald first, though," David said. "We were on the baseball team together in high school," he added for Jim and Eva's benefit.

"I'll come with you," Jennifer told him. "We'll talk later?" she asked Eva.

"I'll be home. I can't wait to take these heels off. My feet are killing me."

David and Jennifer walked together to where Donald was standing slightly off to the side.

David reached out to shake his hand. "I'm so sorry for your loss. How're you holding up?"

"Some days are better than others," Donald replied.

Jennifer placed her hand on Donald's arm, planning to express her sympathy. A jolt ran up her arm—sharp and unmistakably wrong. She pulled back slightly, unsettled. That feeling of misalignment came over her again.

She blinked to regain her composure. It had all happened in just seconds—not long enough for anyone to notice.

"I'm so sorry, too. We're going to miss Terry at the Maple Syrup Weekend," she managed to get out.

"I'm going to fill in for him. It meant a lot to him to be a part of it this year," Donald said, smiling.

Jennifer noticed the smile didn't reach his eyes.

"We should probably go, Dave."

David was about to protest, but stopped when he saw the look in her eyes. He shook Donald's hand again before telling him, "Hang in there, buddy, it will get better."

When they got outside, he took Jennifer's hand. It was ice cold.

"What happened in there?" he asked.

"I'm not sure. Probably nothing," she replied off-handedly.

David looked at her again, but didn't push it. He'd seen that look before and knew she needed time to process whatever it was.

CHAPTER ELEVEN

Annalise considered begging off Jennifer and Eva's invitation to meet them for breakfast the day after the funeral. She'd woken with a headache that lingered even after she'd tried all of her usual home remedies. It wasn't strong enough to send her back to bed; she'd soldiered on before with worse headaches than this. But there was a quality about it that unsettled her. It felt less like pain and more like a mental knocking at a door, as though something was demanding to come through.

As soon as she walked through the door and the familiar scents and sounds of the diner hit her, she was glad she didn't cancel.

"Over here, Lise!"

She turned at the sound of Eva's voice, confused at first. She and Jennifer were sitting at one of the tables instead of "their" usual booth. Then she noticed the booth was already occupied.

"Good morning, ladies," she greeted them and managed a smile that she hoped looked less out-of-sorts to them than she felt.

As if by magic, Betty appeared at Annalise's elbow and set a mug of tea next to her. The distinctive aroma of the Earl Grey tea wafted up and the tension behind Annalise's eyes loosened slightly.

"Do you need a minute to decide?" she asked the group at large.

"We're ready," they replied, nearly in unison.

"So, how was the funeral?" Annalise asked when Betty left to give their orders to the cook.

"Standing room only," Eva replied. "Gregor was there and everybody was treating him like a leper, so Jim and I brought him over to sit with us."

Annalise felt a faint tightening in her chest. She imagined him standing there unsure about whether he belonged, and the loneliness of it brought a tear to her eye—but she blinked it away.

"He told us that the detectives had questioned him," Eva added.

"Doesn't sound like they've got enough evidence to charge him with anything," Annalise reasoned.

"That seems likely. As far as I know, they haven't mentioned exactly how Terry was murdered. They might still be trying to figure that out," Jennifer replied.

Eva gave Annalise a recap of more details about the funeral and reception and Jennifer added what she'd observed.

When they'd finished, Annalise gave Jennifer a scrutinizing look. "You're holding back something."

Jennifer's cheeks flushed a pale shade of pink. "I feel like I just got caught lying by omission to my mom," she teased.

"Are you ready to come clean?" Annalise asked with a smile.

Jennifer paused to collect her thoughts. "I've been trying to put my finger on what's been bothering me ever since the funeral. It's right at the edge of *getting it*, though."

"Maybe we can help you work through it," Eva suggested.

"It's about Donald. I caught him staring at Gregor when he

came to sit with us. He didn't notice me watching him, and I think because of that he wasn't guarding his expression. At first I thought it looked like he was trying to decide if he believed the rumors that Gregor might have killed Terry."

"Considering all the rumors flying around, that's a reasonable conclusion," Eva said.

"But then?" Annalise asked, tapping into how Jennifer had prefaced her observation with the words "at first."

"Well, I can see how that might be what he was thinking, Eva, but it was more than that. He was watching Gregor, but there was no reaction. It was like he was observing, with no emotion." Jennifer paused, her lips pursed and her forehead wrinkled, as she considered her words.

"Detached, maybe?" she said, trying out the word, then shook her head. "That makes it sound temporary. It was… settled. Like whatever he should have been feeling had already come and gone. That probably doesn't make sense either."

Annalise felt the familiar warning—a faint hum just beneath the surface—but Jennifer was still speaking about Terry. Annalise let it pass, knowing better than to interrupt when something important was unfolding.

"There was something in Donald's eyes…" She hesitated, "no, what wasn't in them would be more accurate… We were getting ready to leave and he mentioned filling in for Terry for the festival. He smiled, but only with his mouth. There was no warmth in his eyes. Something about it was off."

Pain spiked behind Annalise's eyes, sharp enough to make her wince. She pressed her fingers between her brows, recognition settling in. The reaction wasn't random—it was insistence. Jennifer had just brushed against something Donald had worked hard to hide.

"That's it," she said softly as her eyes unfocused and she had a faraway look.

Eva and Jennifer looked at each other, the thought *what's she talking about?* passing between them.

Annalise was still working through it in her head. She finally understood why her visions had been blocked. There were no emotions for her to grab onto and demand to be seen. What Jennifer was describing was what came after, once the fire had burned itself out and everything was still.

I've been thinking it had to be someone who was angry enough to commit murder. But what if anger isn't what motivated the killer?

She still didn't have any sense of who murdered Terry, but at least now she could release her preconceptions about them and stop trying to make them fit who *she* thought they were. As she had the thought, all the bands of tension wrapped around her head let go.

Once again, the murmur of conversation at nearby tables, clinking of silverware, and the aromas of food coming from the diner's kitchen penetrated, and she was fully present.

Eva and Jennifer had waited patiently for the moment to pass, knowing the signs of when Annalise was caught in a psychic revelation.

"I think I've been listening for the wrong thing," she said.

"What do you mean?" Eva asked.

Annalise took a sip of her tea and grimaced. It had turned cold.

"I've been waiting for heat."

"Heat?" Jennifer asked. She was looking at Annalise as though she'd lost her mind.

They interrupted their conversation when Betty arrived with their meals. For once, Betty didn't stop to share the day's gossip. Once she'd left, Annalise explained her revelation about the lack of emotions.

"What does that mean for discovering the killer's identity?" Eva asked.

"I don't know—yet."

That had to be enough for now. They picked up their forks and tucked into their meals.

Annalise's thoughts had her completely in their hold. The shadow had been lifted. She couldn't see yet what it had been hiding, but her confidence was back.

CHAPTER TWELVE

On the TV tray beside her, a small pair of scissors, thread, and needle threader, and a plastic container of binding clips were assembled and ready. Eva queued up an audiobook and picked up the table runner.

She'd reached her least favorite part of the project—hand stitching the binding. If it had been just for her, she might have used the sewing machine, but getting the stitching to look seamless still eluded her. Since this was for the auction, only hand stitching would do.

Reuben was curled up on his bed in the bay window, the sun streaming through the window onto him, providing extra warmth.

She'd only sewn down a few inches when her phone rang. Eva glanced at the screen and was surprised to see Phil Robertson's name displayed. A part of her had been expecting the call, but now that it was happening, she felt a ripple of unease low in her belly.

"Good morning, Phil. It's nice to hear from you."

"I wasn't sure if I should, but Dennis and I could use the quilt club ladies' help."

"Let me guess. It's about the Terry Dickinson case," Eva said.

"It is. We were wondering if we could meet with all of you—today, if possible."

"I'll have to check and get back to you. We could meet here if that's okay with you. Does it matter what time?"

"No, we're willing to meet at your convenience."

"I'll call when I've got it set."

It wasn't desperation Eva heard in Phil's voice, but she got the sense that they'd reached a block in their investigation that needed the kind of out-of-the-box help the quilt club could give.

EVA

The detectives want to meet with us. Can you come to my house this afternoon or evening?

SARAH

I'm free later this afternoon. Does 4 work?

JENNIFER

That works. I can't stay long, though.

ANNALISE

4 is good for me, too. Any idea what they want?

EVA

Only that it's about the Terry Dickinson murder.

ANNALISE

~

ARE YOU EXPECTING COMPANY?

"Yes, Reuben. It's a special meeting with the ladies and the detectives," Eva replied, as she picked up a stray thread from the floor and continued to straighten up the living room.

You're not bringing that dog back are you? he demanded.

"Now, Reuben, I thought you and Ginger were friends."

Friends is a strong word. What's the word for someone you tolerate?

Eva stopped her cleaning and thought a moment. "I don't think there is one that fits that. The closest thing to it might be frenemy? I'm not sure if I've got the definition of the portmanteau correct, though."

The what?

"Portmanteau. It refers to a blend of two words to create a new one. Like brunch. It combines breakfast and lunch."

Why didn't you just say frenemy and leave it at that instead of trying to impress me with your fifty cent words? Ginger is my friend sometimes and my enemy others. But you didn't answer my original question. Is that beast coming back?

Eva sighed. "No, Reuben. This has nothing to do with Maggie or Ginger."

Good!

He stalked into the kitchen, leaving Eva shaking her head at Reuben's recalcitrant attitude.

The doorbell rang and Eva gave the room one more scan before going to open the door. Annalise was the first to arrive.

"Mmm. You made banana bread, didn't you?" she asked, inhaling deeply.

"Good nose. I had a few overripe bananas, so this was a perfect opportunity to make banana bread and not end up eating it all myself."

Jennifer and Sarah just arrived, Reuben announced just before the doorbell rang.

"I smell banana bread," Sarah said. "Do you have coffee, too?"

"Do you even have to ask?" Annalise teased. "A get-together at Eva's without coffee is like a Maine winter without snow. It just doesn't happen."

"It's all set up in the dining room. It's got more seating for all of us."

The doorbell chimed again.

"That's probably the detectives. You go on ahead and we'll meet you in there." She opened the door to let the detectives inside.

"Thanks for setting this up, Eva." Dennis Smith said.

"You're most welcome. Everyone's here—follow me."

"It's our favorite detectives," Sarah greeted them before taking her second slice of banana bread and spreading it with butter.

"If you want any of this, you'd better grab it now before Sarah eats it all," Jennifer teased and passed the plate to the men.

"Don't mind if I do," Phil Robertson said, placing a slice on the plate Annalise handed to him.

"Phil and I wanted to talk to you about the Terry Dickinson case," Dennis began, once everyone was settled in with their beverages and bread. "What can you tell us about the relationship between him and Gregor MacHenry?"

"Despite what you might have heard about the fights they'd had before Terry was found, I don't think Gregor had anything to do with his death," Eva replied first. "It's just an opinion, of course, but I've spoken to Gregor a couple times since and he doesn't strike me as someone who committed murder."

"I agree with Eva," Jennifer chimed in. "Gregor has a quick temper, but so did Terry. But when it comes down to it, they were still neighbors who would put aside their differences to help each other."

"What about the property line dispute?" Dennis asked.

"It was never an issue until Terry decided to start his own maple syrup business. The properties have been in their families for generations and I don't know this for sure, but the lots have probably never been surveyed. It wouldn't surprise me to find out Terry honestly thought he was on his own land," Jennifer added.

"Why didn't they have the property surveyed?" Phil asked.

"That's what I said," Sarah replied.

"When you've got that much acreage, it can get expensive. My guess is they didn't want to spend the money," Eva offered.

"What about you Annalise? You've been quiet," Dennis asked. He'd noticed she hadn't added to the conversation, which was unusual.

Annalise shifted in her chair. "I haven't seen Gregor since he found Terry's body and I don't know anything more about the property line dispute."

"That's the in-the-box response. What about your out-of-the-box one?" Dennis asked, grinning.

Annalise smiled. "I don't have one—yet. It's not for lack of trying, but something was blocking me. I *think* I know the reason why, but didn't figure it out until yesterday. I wanted to make things fit instead of listening to what my intuition was trying to tell me."

"All I've heard is that the autopsy determined Terry's death was a homicide, but do they know how he was killed?" Sarah asked.

"Blunt force trauma to the back of the head. There was no blood at the scene so no one was looking for a weapon. Carl Tremblay took some pictures when the body was found, and Ian Nelson did, too, but there was no reason to think they needed a CSI team out there," Dennis replied.

"Even if they did that now, any weapon could have been removed," Phil added. "That's why we were hoping you might have figured out something."

"What can you tell us about Donald Dickinson?" Dennis switched gears.

"He and David were friends in high school, but lost touch when Donald moved away after graduation," Jennifer said. "Dave said there was always some sibling rivalry between him and Terry, but nothing more than usual. Their dad's favorite was Terry and he didn't try to hide it."

Phil took out his notebook and wrote that down. "That checks with what we found out. He's been living in southern Maine, but he told us he'd come to visit Terry recently."

Jennifer's comment about the rivalry and favoritism sparked something for Annalise. *Resentment—not anger. That's the emotion I was missing.* She kept her thoughts to herself, though. She wasn't ready to share them until she'd had a chance to test them out in private.

"Do you know why the property was left just to Terry and not to both of them?" Phil asked Jennifer.

"Dave told me it was because that's how the land had always been handed down. The oldest son inherited it. His father was all about traditions. So, it wasn't just about Terry being the favorite that he's the one who got it when his parents died."

"Do you know who will inherit it now?" Dennis asked.

"No idea. But if Terry didn't have a Will, Donald would be the next in line as the only sibling. Terry was divorced and didn't have any children," Jennifer replied.

Phil made another note.

"I don't suppose you've had any visits from the deceased?" Dennis addressed Sarah.

"I wouldn't have waited this long to tell you if I had," Sarah smiled, softening her words.

Phil hesitated, as if weighing whether to cross a line he couldn't uncross. "Would you be willing to try?"

Sarah groaned. "I was hoping you wouldn't bring that up. I should have known better."

"Doesn't answer the question," Phil continued.

Sarah audibly let out her breath and her shoulders slumped. "Sure." Her voice was resigned.

Phil's voice was soft, "We could really use your help. Without a weapon or clear motive, we don't have a lot to go on. You've been able to speed things up in the past. You're the only one who can give us an eyewitness account."

"You'll have to take me to the scene. I can't go traipsing around in the woods without raising questions. Especially since I don't even live in Glen Lake."

"We can make that happen," Dennis answered. "Could you meet us tomorrow?"

"Could you come with us, too, Jennifer? Maybe there's something out there you can touch and do your thing," Phil said.

It was a testament to the detectives' trust in the women that they asked without any embarrassment about their unconventional methods.

"I think so."

She checked the calendar app on her phone and Sarah did the same.

"If you can do it in the morning, I'm free," Sarah replied.

"Me, too. Doesn't matter what time," Jennifer added.

"Ten o'clock?" Phil asked.

"Sounds good," Jennifer said, and Sarah raised a thumb up as she typed the information into the calendar.

"I think that's all we have for today," Phil said, tucking his notebook back into his jacket's inside pocket. "Thanks for the coffee and banana bread, Eva. We should get back to the office."

Sarah checked her watch. "Me, too. I promised Ashley we'd go out for dinner tonight."

"And I need to get dinner started. I'll follow you out," Jennifer said.

After they'd said their goodbyes, Eva returned to the dining room where Annalise was still sitting.

"Want to talk about it?" she asked.

Annalise smiled. "You know me too well. It's nothing major. I just had an insight when they were talking about Terry and Donald. Remember what I said yesterday about listening for the wrong thing?"

Eva nodded.

"Now I know what I should be listening for."

CHAPTER THIRTEEN

The day was warm for March and the snow was turning to slush. Their boots left deep impressions in the remaining snow and the ground exposed below them turned muddy as the four tromped into the woods. Phil and Dennis led the way, followed by Sarah, and Jennifer tagged along at the rear of the line.

They'd met at Terry's and took the path he'd made walking from his house to the maple grove. They were all silent in deference to Sarah in case Terry attempted to make contact.

Jennifer followed slowly, scanning the ground and tree branches in case anything appeared that looked out of place, but so far, she hadn't spotted anything unusual.

Even before Phil and Dennis stopped walking, Sarah knew they were close to where the murder had taken place. A low humming sound began in her ears and she felt Terry's presence.

"He's here," she announced, her voice soft.

Everyone stopped in their tracks. It didn't surprise them that they didn't see anyone. They'd all witnessed Sarah interacting with ghosts and knew that not all appearances were visible to anyone other than her.

"Terry, my name is Sarah Pascal. I'm here to talk to you about what happened the day you died."

He always wanted what wasn't his.

Sarah turned slowly in a circle. She couldn't see where the voice was coming from, but wasn't discouraged. Sometimes it took longer for a ghost to appear, but even without seeing them, as long as she could hear their message, all was not lost.

"Can you tell me what happened that day? Do you know who struck you?"

Came out in the morning to check my sap lines. Gregor's been messing with them. Says they're on his land.

His voice had taken on a tone of indignation and the fuzzy image of a man began to materialize.

This land has belonged to my family for generations.

"That's what I've been told," Sarah said, keeping her voice even, not wanting to escalate emotions before she could ask about who committed the murder. "What else do you remember?"

No one had messed with the lines so I was walking back to my house. He popped out of the woods, real surprised to see me.

Sarah's pulse quickened with excitement that the mystery could be solved in the next few minutes.

"Who was it?"

Dad should've told me first. Never would have given it to him.

Sarah's brow furrowed. Not only wasn't it the answer she'd hoped for; it sounded like a completely different conversation.

"Never would have given what to him?"

None of your business!

"Sorry, I didn't mean to intrude. Can you tell me who you were talking to? On that day?" Sarah clarified. She didn't want him thinking she was asking about today.

I got angry and told him he'd better give it back. He found it on MY land. I started walking back to the house, and that's the last thing I remember.

Sarah stifled the frustration she felt and gently asked again, "I don't know who you were talking to. Can you tell me who it was? The police don't know who killed you and they could use your…"

All she heard was muttering, but the words were unintelligible. It was as though he'd already stopped listening to her. The humming sound in her ears silenced and Terry's image disappeared along with it.

"Darn it!" she exclaimed, no longer worried about expressing her frustration.

The others were looking on expectantly, unsure whether it was safe to speak.

"It wasn't a complete waste of time," Sarah began, "but it's not the information you were hoping for." She gave them the salient information about her exchange with Terry.

"Any idea what he meant about giving it back?" Dennis asked.

"Was he talking about the syrup?" Phil asked, his inflection raising as though he couldn't believe the confrontation had been about that.

Sarah paused, playing the conversation back in her head. "Possibly, but my gut is telling me that wasn't it. It's something completely unrelated."

"Do you have a guess?" Phil asked.

"No, but I don't think Terry was angry with Gregor in that moment. He said his *dad* should have told him first. This feels like it's family-related, not neighbors."

Phil and Dennis exchanged glances.

"Sounds like we need to dig deeper into Donald Dickinson," Dennis said.

Jennifer had been standing off to the side, only half-listening to the conversation. A beam of sunlight reflected off something half-buried in the snow near a tree trunk. Its glimmer caught her attention, and she walked over to investigate.

She knelt down to look closer and recognized it as something curved and metallic and reached out to wiggle it free. As soon as her fingers touched it, a feeling of possessiveness overwhelmed her and she heard a male voice—*It's mine!*

Then she had the sensation of an argument between two men —but not words or faces. It was an emotional impression rather than being a witness to the scene. She felt panic emanating from one of them and fear that what she was holding would be taken away.

Sarah became aware that Jennifer wasn't merely looking at something on the ground and knew immediately what was happening. The detectives followed her eyes and stood quietly, waiting for the moment to pass.

Jennifer shook her head, releasing the last hold the vision had on her and stood with the object in her palm.

"What is it?" Dennis asked.

Jennifer turned the object over in her hand and rubbed it with her thumb and forefinger to remove the mud obscuring some of the surface.

"It's a coin. And it's old." She looked up at the others and held out her palm for them to see.

"Is this what they were fighting about?" Phil asked, addressing them both.

Sarah and Jennifer locked eyes, but neither of them had any certainty about an answer.

"Could be, I suppose," Jennifer replied first. "It's old, but I can't tell how old. The date is worn away, and it's hard to read."

"Doesn't seem like that would be worth fighting over to the point of killing someone," Sarah offered.

"Could be nothing," Phil addressed Dennis. "Should we bag it, anyway? Might turn out to be evidence."

Dennis nodded. "Yeah, I think we should. Just in case."

Phil reached into his inside jacket pocket and took out a clear evidence bag and held it out to Jennifer. She dropped the coin inside, but regretted having to do so.

With the coin turned over, she wouldn't be able to get anything more from it later. And there *was* something more. She didn't know what, but her intuition was strong that it held more secrets.

It's not just the coin. There's something about that location, too, she thought. *I'm going to need another way—another chance to discover what they're trying to tell me.*

CHAPTER FOURTEEN

Sarah and Jennifer lingered after Phil and Dennis drove away.

"What's your intuition telling you about the coin?" Sarah asked.

"It's fuzzy, but I think the coin is definitely related to Terry's murder. What you heard about Terry saying his dad should have told him first makes sense to me. The coin adds more context. Why it was out here in the woods, though, I haven't got a clue. Maybe if I'd had a little longer with it, I could have gotten a better connection."

"That's not going to happen now."

"No," Jennifer agreed, sounding discouraged. "Do you think Terry would appear to you again?" Jennifer asked.

"Possibly, but I don't think it will be today. Not unless he follows me home. I have a project for my day job I need to finish."

"I should get going, too."

The women each went their separate ways but even once she'd arrived home, Jennifer couldn't stop thinking about the coin and the emotions she'd felt when she held it. Strongest was the fear of having it taken away, and taking into account Terry's words, she was sure the person holding the coin hadn't been him.

Underneath that was a strong sense of resentment—definitely coming from the man holding it. And a sense of entitlement because he—and she knew it was a he—hadn't been treated fairly. The coin was compensation for not getting his fair share.

She closed her eyes to attempt recapturing her experience in the woods, but felt nothing new. She needed a physical connection to an object for that to happen.

If only I'd been allowed to keep the coin a little longer, Jennifer mused, but knew she'd done the right thing turning it over to the detectives. They needed a clean chain of evidence just in case it became instrumental in prosecuting the case once the murderer was found.

What had unsettled her most, wasn't the resentment—it was the certainty behind it. Whoever had been holding the coin hadn't acted on impulse. He'd believed he was righting a wrong. And he'd been willing to kill to do that.

Jennifer opened her eyes, a chill slowly working its way down her spine.

CHAPTER FIFTEEN

Annalise rested the book she'd been unsuccessfully reading in her lap. Her mind kept drifting back to her revelation that she'd blocked herself from seeing more because she'd misinterpreted the emotions of the killer.

Her chest tightened as doubt overtook her and she became aware of how much it had shaken her confidence that she could trust any new visions.

"That's what he's doing," she said, at last. "He's able to misdirect the investigation because his demeanor is so convincing."

Annalise already suspected who the killer might be. It wasn't that she'd seen nothing. It was that she'd dismissed what she felt because it didn't fit. She'd been thinking instead of listening.

She sat with that for a moment before deciding, "I'm not going to let him get the better of me." Her voice was strong, and she felt a sense of conviction that this time she'd keep herself open to all possibilities.

She placed the book that had grown heavy in her hands on the table beside her chair, then rested her hands in her lap, closed her eyes, and let her mind empty. It took longer than usual, but an image began to form.

A man's hands holding a book—*a diary*, she realized. The words were written in a tight cursive—the word stingy popped into Annalise's thoughts. A hand-drawn map was spread out in front of him. He made a mark on the map and folded it, then placed it inside the diary.

The scene jumped and Annalise saw a grove of trees as the man moved with no hesitation to his destination. In his hand was a shovel. In the periphery, buckets hung from trees but Annalise sensed this area was not part of the sap operation.

He knows exactly where he's going, she thought.

He moved quietly through the woods, the powder snow muffling his steps. The only sound was the occasional chick-a-dee-dee-dee song of a chickadee perched on a branch overhead.

This time Annalise sensed a calm, focused determination. It contrasted with the anger she'd expected before and she knew she was on the right track this time. She wasn't projecting the emotions of the man to fit her expectations; she was letting his feelings come through.

The man stopped at a spot where a large boulder stood. He kneeled down to inspect the rock. To anyone who didn't have the map, the X that had been etched into the rock could easily be dismissed as a natural formation.

He scraped away the top layer of snow and began to dig. He hadn't gone far when she heard a metallic ping and felt the man's satisfaction—*it's mine now*. He cleared more dirt away and knelt down. The lid of a metal container with a handle on top was resting in the hole. He took the handle and wiggled the box carefully to remove it.

He opened the lid to reveal a cache of silver coins. He removed one to examine it and then his head shot up as though he'd heard something. Annalise felt her own pulse quicken, sharing his sense of alertness, but then felt a sense of calm as he methodically carried on to cover his tracks.

He quickly closed the lid and placed the box back in the hole, then filled it back in with the dirt and snow he'd removed. The man slipped the coin in his pocket and retraced his steps.

The image faded and Annalise sat quietly, immersing herself in the details of the vision and a new perception of the man came through.

This was someone who believed he'd been entitled to the treasure he'd found. He'd been deprived of an inheritance that should have belonged to him and this was a small compensation. The resentment he hid under the surface came through clearly.

Annalise knew that in his mind, he had righted a wrong that had been done. It hadn't been his intention to kill, but what choice did he have? It would have all been taken away otherwise. Terry deserved what he got.

She opened her eyes and shivered, unsettled by the emotion he felt. This was someone who could appear calm, polite, unassuming. She'd been wrong about the heat—the anger—this was cold, calculating—and dangerous.

CHAPTER SIXTEEN

"*I* saw Gregor at The Checkout yesterday. He's still not himself. He said hello, but it wasn't his usual greeting and he didn't stick around to talk," Eva mentioned at the beginning of the next Quilts Club meeting.

"It seems like most of the suspicion has died down that he was involved in Terry's murder, but it has to have left a bad taste in his mouth to think people in town even thought he would be capable of it," Jennifer added.

"From what you've told me about him, it didn't sound like Gregor was a homicidal maniac, so it's surprising that even people who know him turned on him so easily. Unfortunately, that happens more often than it should when people get scared," Sarah said, her tone thoughtful.

"That's true, Sarah." Eva looked over at Annalise who had remained quiet during the conversation. "Are you okay, Annalise? You look like you've got something on your mind."

"Remember I'd said at our last meeting that I was looking for the wrong emotion? I'd let my head do the thinking that whoever did this had to have been angry with Terry."

The others nodded in acknowledgement.

"I tried again, but set those preconceptions aside. The last time I tried it all felt murky, and I wasn't getting sharp images. This time it was as though all the pieces snapped together and I got something else—a motive. I'm ninety-nine percent sure I know who the killer is."

"You do?" Eva asked. The surprise on her face was mirrored on Jennifer and Sarah's.

Jennifer felt a sense of apprehension, as though she guessed what Annalise was about to say.

"Yes, but let me start at the beginning and tell you my vision." She recounted the details and ended with how it tied into Jennifer's discovery of the coin and Sarah's encounter with Terry. "The only person I can think of who would fit all of this is Donald."

There was a hush in the room as everyone considered that possibility.

"I think you said out loud what we all were thinking," Eva said, breaking the silence.

"Me, too," Jennifer agreed.

"I had an inkling of going in that direction after my encounter with Terry, but I don't know enough about the family history to be certain about it. I think I'm going to have to try again, but there's no way I'm going to go out there by myself," Sarah said.

"Absolutely not," Annalise said, her voice firm. "When the vision ended, one thing stayed with me: Donald believes he is entitled to that treasure." She paused briefly. "And he was justified in killing Terry."

Sarah's eyebrows rose at this declaration and Annalise noticed.

"I don't think it was premeditated," she clarified. "But he feels he was cheated out of his inheritance and when Terry stood in his way of getting all the coins, he thought that was his only option. What I felt was resentment, and a sense of being justified to protect what he thought was his."

Annalise's words resonated with what Jennifer had felt when she held the coin and her reaction at the funeral when she'd touched Donald's arm. "Do you think the coin I found in the woods was from the cache you saw in your vision?" she asked.

Annalise considered the possibility, waiting for internal feedback. "Yes. I didn't see that happen specifically in my vision, but that doesn't mean he put all the coins back before burying them again. My intuition is telling me it had to be connected to Donald for you to have had the response you did when you picked it up."

"So where does that leave us with going back to try to make contact with Terry again?" Sarah asked.

"We should probably bring Phil and Dennis in on this anyway," Eva suggested. "They should be the ones to go with you, for a number of reasons."

"I agree. Should we call them now?" Annalise asked.

"I think so." Eva said, picking up her phone where it lay on the table. "I'm putting it on speaker."

"Hello, Eva."

"I have you on speaker, Phil. I'm here with Jennifer, Sarah, and Annalise and we have some new information to share with you about the Dickinson case."

"Is it the kind I can put in a report or the kind I keep in my back pocket?"

"The latter. I'm going to let Annalise take over now."

Annalise repeated her vision for Phil and included her insights about the emotional texture of what she'd seen and her suspicions about Donald.

"And we were wondering if you could take me back to the crime scene?" Sarah added as soon as Annalise was done. "Maybe asking Terry about this will get more out of him."

"It might be best to hold back that Donald is suspected as being his attacker. Even though this isn't admissible in court, I'd feel better about not leading the witness, so to speak." Phil said the last part with a touch of humor.

"That makes sense. I'm sure I can figure out a way to ask questions about his killer's identity. I could just ask if he knew who it was again. He never answered me the first time, but maybe it will get him to tell me if I explain we need his help finding his killer or they might get away with it," Sarah suggested.

"It's worth a shot," Phil agreed.

They made plans to meet the next day.

"I hope I'm right," Annalise said quietly. "Otherwise, we could be pointing the finger at another innocent person. Just like what's happened with Gregor."

"What if Donald has already taken the coins? He's had time to go back," Eva wondered aloud.

"Donald is still here, even though he could have returned home by now. That makes me think he still has unfinished business—getting the rest of the coins." Jennifer stated.

"But he could say it had nothing to do with Terry's murder even if he gets caught with them," Eva suggested.

"It's up to us to find a way to get him to confess. Pretty much like all of the cases we've solved," Sarah reminded her.

They all knew the truth of her words and for the moment, there was nothing more they could do.

CHAPTER SEVENTEEN

*S*arah, Jennifer and the detectives met the next day at Terry's house. After speaking with Phil and Dennis the night before, the Club agreed it would make sense for Jennifer to come, too. There might be another coin that had been hidden in the snow or some other item that would trigger a new revelation.

There was less snow than the previous visit after a week of warmer weather. The taps and buckets had been pulled from the maple trees and there was a sense of expectation in the air. Some of it the promise of spring around the corner, and the rest the group's optimism that more would be revealed if Sarah made contact with Terry.

"I'm glad I decided to wear boots today," Dennis said as they tromped down the now muddy path to the crime scene.

"It's mud season a little early this year," Jennifer replied.

"Don't get too sure about that. April can still be a snow month," Phil cautioned.

"What a killjoy!" Sarah teased, speaking over her shoulder to Phil and the others walking behind her.

"That's my middle name," Phil retorted with a smile.

The sun was warm, shining in a brilliant blue sky. As they

walked farther into the forest, they each unzipped their jackets almost as if they'd choreographed it.

As they approached the spot where Terry had been found, Sarah felt a heaviness in the air and knew Terry was nearby. She paused and held up her finger to let the others know she wanted to tune into her awareness. They understood and waited while she walked a few steps ahead to focus.

As she did, Terry's specter began to solidify. Sarah noticed a change in his demeanor. The anger was gone, and he appeared subdued.

You came back.

"Yes. We were hoping you'd be willing to talk to me again."

Well, go ahead then. Say what you came to say.

"Thank you for talking to me." Sarah had role-played her questions the night before with Ashley, hoping this time she wouldn't antagonize Terry. "I want to reassure you that we're only here to help. We want to find your killer and bring them to justice."

Terry nodded slowly, his eyes appraising Sarah.

Taking that as a positive sign, Sarah continued. "You mentioned you were arguing with someone that day. Someone had something that you thought belonged to you."

Terry stood taller and pulled his shoulders back in a defiant stance. Sarah's breath caught at the gesture, worried she'd gone too far. She reminded herself that pushing too hard could make him disappear again, but this might be her only chance. Her shoulders relaxed when Terry spoke again.

That's right. My dad left me this land and as far as I'm concerned, that included anything that was on it or buried in it. My brother told me it was finders keepers. He found it and that meant it was his.

"Can you tell me what it was?" Sarah held her breath. She and Ashley had discussed whether this might set Terry off again, but in the end, agreed it was important to tie the coins to their argument.

Terry eyed her suspiciously for a moment and Sarah could see he was debating whether to answer.

I'd given him a box with some junk of Dad's that had one of his old diaries. If I'd known what it said, I never would have done that. He said it with a tone of regret and bitterness that he'd misjudged its importance.

Sarah waited patiently for him to continue.

He'd written about some treasure of coins buried a long time ago and that he'd tried to find, but never did. Donald figured it out, and I caught him trying to sneak away with it. He gave some of them to me, but then he came back again for the rest of it. I didn't know there was more.

"Was Donald trying to take them the day you argued?"

Sarah felt the group in the background tensing with anticipation. They could only hear her side of the conversation, but she'd phrased the question to let them know she was about to learn if the coins and the argument were connected.

That's right. I didn't even know he was there and I don't think he expected to see me either. He was looking at a coin when he came out of the woods and didn't notice me at first. I was so mad I could spit, but I didn't want to fight about it there. I just told him to give it back and started walking back to the house. Like I said before, that's the last thing I remember. One minute I was walking along and then everything went black.

Terry's head drooped and his expression turned sad, as though he'd had a change of heart.

Maybe I should have just let him have them. I got the land, and he didn't really get much of anything when Dad died.

Sarah hesitated before asking her next question but Terry's presence was beginning to become transparent and she knew she wouldn't have much time.

"Was there anyone else there that day or was it just you and Donald?"

Terry looked up, meeting Sarah's eyes. He understood what was implied and for a moment, Sarah didn't think he would answer. She saw the conflict on his face. Even though it would mean his killer might go free, Terry was reluctant to blame his brother.

There could have been. Terry's tone was defiant. *Gregor is right next door, and he's been poking around and accusing me of stealing sap, but I still say those trees are on my land.*

"Did you see Gregor?"

No, but... Terry's eyes narrowed. *You're just trying to trick me into blaming my brother. I'm not going to do that. We're done.*

Sarah groaned as she felt Terry's presence disappear. She turned to face the others.

"I'm sorry. I pushed too hard."

She filled them in on the side of the conversation they hadn't been able to hear.

"It's not a total loss," Dennis reassured her. "Now we have his substantiation that Donald was here with him that day. It gives us something to question Donald about."

"How are we supposed to do that? We can't exactly say Terry told us about the coins," Phil pointed out.

"But we do have the coin that Jennifer found. We can ask him if he knew anything about it. He might deny it, but we can press him on it."

Phil still appeared skeptical.

"I know it's going to take some more investigating, but we've been in this spot before," Dennis tried to reassure him.

"We'll see," Phil replied, still not convinced.

Jennifer had remained quiet during their exchange. As they'd been talking, she'd felt a pull to a spot deeper into the woods.

"Are you okay?" Sarah asked her when she noticed Jennifer's attention was drawn away from them.

"I'm fine, but..." She stopped as the feeling receded and second-guessed she'd felt anything unusual. "It's nothing," she said, forcing a smile. But a part of her questioned whether it really was her imagination. It had felt so strong for just long enough to feel real.

Sarah studied her, but didn't push it.

"Donald still hasn't left town. That might mean he's waiting for the right time to come back to get the rest of the coins," Dennis said.

"If they're still there," Phil said.

"You sure are a gloomy Gus today, pal," Dennis teased.

"It's the case. Seems like we're not getting anywhere and it's frustrating. We're pretty sure it's got to be Donald, but we have nothing to pin on him," Phil explained.

Dennis nodded. "I get it, but don't give up. For now, though, we might as well wrap it up here. We'll keep an eye on Donald. He's bound to slip up and in the meantime, we'll do what we can to find some evidence to tie him to the murder."

Phil sighed. "I guess that's all we can do. Let's go, ladies. Show's over."

They walked back through the woods with Jennifer the last to go. The magnetic draw she'd felt earlier returned, and she stared into the woods, but nothing seemed out of place. She couldn't shake the feeling, though, that something was still unfinished there.

CHAPTER EIGHTEEN

"Are you sure you're okay?" Sarah asked Jennifer when they reached the driveway. "You seem distracted."

"I thought it was just my imagination, but I've got the feeling that there's something out there we're meant to find. It felt like something was trying to lead me farther into the woods."

Phil and Dennis turned back when they realized Sarah and Jennifer were standing at the edge of the path.

"What's up?" Dennis asked.

Sarah nodded at Jennifer to encourage her to speak up.

"I think the coins might still be out there. Or at least some of them." She looked from Dennis to Phil. "I think we should go back."

This time it was their turn to exchange glances. Phil shrugged his shoulders. "Better to rule it out now than come back again later."

They retraced their steps to the maple grove and Jennifer slowly circled the perimeter of the clearing until a disturbance in the air stopped her. The sensation of a magnet pulling her into the woods returned, and she walked toward it. The detectives and Sarah followed behind.

Jennifer scanned the ground and trees, not sure what exactly she was looking for, but trusted she'd know when she found it. She remembered Annalise mentioning a boulder where the coins were buried and set her sights on finding that. It didn't take long before she spotted it.

"I think that's it," she said pointing to the large rock—a remnant of the ancient glacier that had shaped the landscape.

"I remember now. Annalise said it was buried by a boulder," Sarah exclaimed.

They all picked up their pace and found the spot where the ground had obviously been disturbed. Leaves and pine needles had been scattered around it, but didn't fit how nature would have arranged them.

Dennis knelt down and brushed away the debris and the signs of a hole having been covered up were even more obvious. He looked up at Phil. "Should we see what's there?"

Phil hesitated briefly. "I think we'd be safe. It's still related to the crime scene. Must be our lucky day because I've got a shovel in the trunk. I'll be right back."

Five minutes later he returned with the shovel and dug into the dirt.

"Wait. We should take a video of this," Dennis said and took out his phone.

The ground had thawed even more, and it was an easy task to remove it. They heard a clink as the shovel met the metal box, making everyone smile.

Phil dug the shovel in deeper, wiggling it under the box and scooping it out. He handed Dennis a pair of latex gloves from his inner pocket. "Brought these along just in case. I've got a few evidence bags, too." He put on his own pair of gloves and waited for Dennis.

Dennis put on the gloves and set his phone up to continue filming. "I'm ready. Go ahead and open the box. I can't believe there's no lock on it."

"Me, too. I guess it is our lucky day after all." Phil opened the box as the others hovered around, each holding their breath.

Inside were silver coins like the one Jennifer had found earlier. He counted the coins and placed them into evidence bags as Dennis continued filming. When all the coins had been removed, Dennis ended the video.

"Can I hold one?" Jennifer asked once she knew it was safe to speak without being part of the video. She and Sarah had prudently stepped back so they would be out of camera range.

Phil grinned as he took another pair of gloves from his pocket and handed them to her.

She returned the smile and after putting on the gloves, took the coin Phil handed to her.

She immediately felt a jolt and closed her eyes to focus. A few minutes later she opened them and handed the coin back to Phil.

"Did you get anything?" Sarah asked.

"I didn't actually *see* anything. It was more like I was getting impressions of what the person was seeing and feeling. I assume it was Donald, but I can't say that with certainty. He was trying to move the coins quickly because he was afraid of being seen. Then he heard a sound like someone walking nearby and he started to panic."

She paused to formulate how to describe what she'd felt. "He was upset that he might be interrupted but determined that he would eventually get all of the coins. He put most of them back but kept one. It was like having a security blanket." She stopped again, blushing a faint shade of red. "I guess that's the mom in me coming out, but that's the impression that came through— like when my kids wouldn't let go of their favorite stuffed animal."

Phil's face drooped—his earlier doubt about their success returning. "It still doesn't prove Donald is the one who was here. Or that he's the murderer."

"But it does prove opportunity and motive if he thought Terry was going to take them away again," Dennis replied. "I still believe we're going to nail him for this. The ladies haven't let us down yet, have they?" he cajoled.

Phil shuffled his feet, embarrassed he might have insulted Sarah and Jennifer.

"No. They've always given us what we need to solve the cases we've worked on together."

"I can check Donald's financials and see if anything shows up that might tie him to the coins," Sarah offered. "Maybe that would at least give you a reason to question him about them."

Phil brightened. "That could work. Thanks!"

"Should we be looking anywhere else?" Dennis asked Jennifer.

"I don't think so. The pull I'd felt faded when we got here and I'm not feeling anything at all now."

"In that case, let's go. We should get these into evidence," Dennis said.

Sarah and Jennifer walked together following the detectives, each lost in their thoughts.

Sarah reached out to Jennifer to catch her attention. "That was a good job you did. Don't let Phil's reaction discourage you," she said softly, not wanting Phil to overhear.

Jennifer smiled gratefully. "Thanks. You, too. We might not have been able to prove it's Donald, but at least we have someone who's a person of interest now."

"That's more than we had a couple days ago," Sarah agreed.

Jennifer nodded, but the sense of relief she'd expected never quite arrived.

Whoever had buried the coins hadn't done it out of greed alone. There had been fear there, too—fear of losing something he believed was already his.

And fear, Jennifer knew, sometimes made people do things they'd sworn they never would.

CHAPTER NINETEEN

"*L*ooks like winter hasn't given up yet, Max."

Max followed Sarah's eyes to the window where outside the sky was gray. The spring-like temperatures of the day before were gone, and snow was spitting in the sky, reminding Mainers that March was a month of contradictions. *In like a lion, and out like a lamb*, went the old proverb, but the time in between didn't progress in a straight line from winter to spring.

Woof, he replied.

"I don't think we'll be taking a walk today."

It wasn't just the weather, though, that made Sarah decide to give up the walk. It felt wrong to take more time away from figuring out a way to directly tie Donald into the murder.

Max gave her his best sad eyes and let out a soft whine.

Sarah felt a twinge of guilt. *Maybe a half hour wouldn't hurt* —but it couldn't be now, she realized.

"Sorry, buddy. I've got work to do."

When Max realized his sad face wasn't going to work, he laid his head on his paws and exhaled a huff of air.

Sarah was about to begin checking through Donald's financials when the phone rang. She picked up the phone and checked the caller ID to make sure it was worth taking the time for the interruption. She answered the call when she saw it was Eva.

"Hello, Eva. How's it going? Is it snowing there too?"

"Just spitting. I called to see how it went yesterday."

"I'm glad we decided to go yesterday. It would have been miserable today. I was able to make contact with Terry, and Jennifer found a cache of coins just like the one she found earlier."

"Really?" Eva asked, surprised. "How did that happen?"

Sarah described yesterday's events for Eva.

"That's amazing! I wonder how long they've been buried there. And who buried them in the first place?" Eva asked when Sarah had finished her recitation.

"I'm just reading between the lines with what Terry said and Annalise's vision, but I don't think it was Donald. And the coins are old," Sarah offered.

"That makes sense. It doesn't seem like it would have anything to do with Gregor, either."

"That's a good point," Sarah agreed.

"Where does that leave us now?" Eva asked

"I was just about to begin looking through Donald's financials to see if there's any way to connect the coins to him when you called."

"In that case, I'll leave you to it. Let me know if you find anything interesting."

"I'll be sure to do that."

Sarah began examining Donald's financial records, but a half hour later, she sat back in her chair, disappointed. Nothing stood out. If anything, Donald's financials were boring.

The same income from his job and expenses for rent, utilities, groceries, credit cards that he never maxed out, and other mundane costs of living appeared month after month with little to no variation. Sarah thought about what a structured life

Donald was living—and how little joy or rewards he gave himself. *How sad and lonely his life must be if this is how he's living it*, she thought.

She was about to admit defeat, but her intuition nudged her to look one more time. Still nothing.

"There's got to be more," she declared—frustrated, but not ready to give up yet. Or to admit she might be on a wild goose chase.

Sarah thought for a moment and then decided to expand her search and hacked her way into Donald's emails. She scanned down the list in his Inbox and her eyes paused on one that seemed out of the ordinary. She almost decided to ignore it, but felt a quiet insistence to keep digging.

The subject line was Professional Services—invoice attached. She checked the sender's email address and something about the name triggered a memory. She sat with that for a moment, her face scowling in concentration. *Why does that sound so familiar?*

She was about to scroll past the email and then it came to her. The company was an appraisal service. It didn't have "appraiser" in the name, which had thrown her off, but she'd come across it in work for another client.

Relieved that she'd remembered, she opened the e-mail. This could be just what she'd been searching for.

The invoice attached to the e-mail was for a modest amount. But what set her pulse racing was the description of the item being appraised. It matched the coins they'd found at the crime scene.

She went back to Donald's financials and found a corresponding payment. But there still was nothing that indicated he had sold the coin.

Sarah stared at the screen, tapping her fingers on her desk as she considered why Donald had taken the coins, but hadn't sold them. And then it struck her.

He didn't want cash. He wanted confirmation.

She began to connect the dots. Terry got the land. Donald got nothing. That matched what she'd learned about Donald from her conversations with Terry, and Annalise and Jennifer's impressions about him.

She tested out another theory:

Terry had given him the diary that led to Donald discovering the coins. Donald believed the coins were the one thing that rightfully belonged to him. *Finders keepers.*

That felt right. At least they had a motive for why he took the coins.

That was only part of the equation, though. The appraisal proved Donald's knowledge of the existence of the coins. But it still didn't connect him to Terry's murder. It was only circumstantial, but might be enough to open the door to allow Phil and Dennis to bring Donald in for an interrogation.

Still not enough to officially count him as a person of interest, but it might rattle him. That could go either way if what Annalise had felt was on point about his resentment.

She debated whether to call them immediately. Time might be running out to prove Donald was Terry's killer. In the end, she decided to wait until she could do more research into the case. She'd almost skipped past the appraisal, and the thought allowed more doubts to creep in.

What if she'd missed something else? Or, what if she was wrong about Donald's motives? If they called him in too early to ask questions, would that tip him off and he'd make a run for it?

She looked back at her screen and the appraisal. The appraisal payment sat there beside it—small and undeniable.

It confirmed that this wasn't about money. It was about what Donald believed had been taken from him. And what he was willing to take back.

The quiet of the house felt suffocating. Max lifted his head as if sensing her unease and uttered a soft *woof* before trotting over to her and licking her hand.

Sarah smiled, grateful for the comforting gesture. She looked outside and saw the weather had changed yet again. The sun was shining now.

"What do you think, Max? Are you ready to take that walk now?"

His tail wagged furiously, and he ran to the spot where his leash was hanging, then brought it back to Sarah.

A few minutes later, they were outside enjoying the fresh air and exercise, but the uneasy feeling she'd had lingered. This was the point in their investigations where it moved from investigation to possible danger. And Sarah knew she'd need to be on guard.

CHAPTER TWENTY

The walk helped clear Sarah's head. By the time she and Max returned home, she was ready to call Phil and Dennis about the appraisal. She first emailed them the document and the proof of Donald's payment and followed up with a call.

"Phil, it's Sarah," she announced when he picked up. "I just sent you and Dennis an email. Is it in your Inbox yet?"

"Just a sec. I'm putting you on speaker so Dennis can hear."

Sarah waited and then heard Dennis's hello. In the background, she heard Phil telling Dennis to check his email.

"We've got it," Phil said a minute later. "I'm not going to ask you how you got it."

"I know you can't submit this in court, but the description on the appraisal proves Donald had at least one of the coins not long before Terry died," Sarah said. "I know it won't prove he killed him, but maybe it can still be useful."

"I see where you're going with it," Dennis replied. "What do you think, Phil? Is it worth bringing him in for more questioning?"

"It's worth a shot. It might shake him up if he knows we've got the ones we found by the boulder," Phil replied.

"Did you find anything else when you were looking through his financials?" Dennis asked.

"Nothing, he's squeaky clean. I had a thought about what his motive might have been, though," Sarah offered.

"What's that?" Phil asked.

"I don't think he did it just for the money. This is about proving himself… or proving *to* himself might be a better way of putting it… that he deserved to be part of the family legacy. Terry wasn't the only one who mattered even if their dad gave him the land."

"Not sure I get what you mean," Dennis said.

"I do," Phil interjected. "We can use that in our interrogation. Maybe not this next one, but we'll know when the time is right. I'll explain it to you after we hang up."

"Thanks, Sarah. We appreciate the assist, as always," Dennis told her.

"Glad I could help. Let me know what happens, if you can," she replied.

"Will do," Dennis said.

After they'd disconnected the call, Phil explained what Sarah had meant about Donald.

"Okay, now I get it," Dennis said, nodding his head. "Should we call him in now?"

"Yes, the sooner the better." Phil scrolled through his notes and found Donald's phone number.

"Mr. Dickinson, this is Detective Robertson. My partner and I wondered if you could come to the station. We have a few questions we'd like to ask regarding your brother's death. Just trying to make sure we have our facts straight." Phil purposely kept the request as ambiguous as possible so as not to tip Donald off.

"I'm happy to help. When should I come in?" Donald asked,

his voice calm and with no hint of suspicion about the nature of the call.

"Could you be here by three thirty?"

"Yes, that wouldn't be any problem. I'm still staying at my house … my brother's house …" he corrected quickly, but Phil noticed, "so it shouldn't take long to get there."

"We'll see you then," Phil replied, and disconnected the call.

Dennis had waited to make sure the line was closed before saying, "Let's try to reel in a fish."

DONALD ARRIVED PROMPTLY at three-thirty and Phil ushered him into one of the interview rooms where Dennis was waiting.

He looks confident and not the least bit suspicious this is anything but routine, Phil thought.

Dennis rose to greet Donald and after shaking hands they all sat down to business.

"Thanks again for coming in, Mr. Dickinson. As I mentioned, we just have a few questions for you. Can you tell me again where you were the day your brother died?" Phil asked.

"I was on my way to Glen Lake to visit my brother. We hadn't seen each other for a few months, so I'd decided it was a good time to drive north."

"Was that the only reason you came to Glen Lake?" Dennis asked.

"Yes. I moved to southern Maine decades ago. I lost touch with schoolmates growing up. Terry is—was—my only tie to the area."

Phil feigned looking through his notes for his next question. "You were notified of his death by Officer Tremblay?"

"That's right," Donald answered, but his body language indicated he was growing tired of the repetition of being asked for basic information he'd already given to the police.

"When do you plan to return to southern Maine?" Dennis asked. "In case we need to speak with you again in person?"

"I'll need to be here at least a few more days to meet with a local lawyer regarding the probate of Terry's estate."

"Who would that be?" Phil asked.

"I'm using Dylan Johnson. His office is in Glen Lake so that makes it convenient for me. And I know Dylan from when I lived here."

Phil and Dennis exchanged a subtle glance. They knew Dylan, too. They'd been the lead homicide detectives when Dylan had been the suspect in the murder of his partner, Caleb Mitchell. It was also a case they'd worked on with the Quilts Club ladies. They had been instrumental in helping to close the case and exonerate Dylan.

Phil wrote Dylan's name on the case notes, more as a diversion for Donald since they already knew how to contact Dylan.

Dennis and Phil met each other's eyes and Phil nodded. They'd already agreed that Dennis would be the one to bring up the coins. He opened the file in front of him to remove the first coin they'd submitted into evidence. It was in an evidence bag which he slid over to Donald as he and Phil watched carefully for his reaction.

Donald's eyes flickered slightly, but he maintained his composure.

"This was found in the clearing where your brother's body was discovered. Can you tell us anything about it?" Dennis asked.

"May I?" Donald asked waiting for Dennis's permission before picking up the bag to inspect it.

"It's one that belonged to my family. I think Terry had it in his possession. Perhaps he dropped it," Donald suggested and then slid the bag back to Dennis.

"Did you ever have possession of a coin like this?" Dennis asked.

"No, it was Terry's," Donald replied.

"The coins were all in your brother's possession?" Dennis asked.

Donald blinked when he heard the word "coins," but kept his face blank.

"I would have no idea. He didn't share that with me."

"You had a coin evaluated recently. This one matches the coin you had appraised."

A small bead of sweat appeared on Donald's forehead. "Well, yes, Terry asked me to get it appraised."

"So, you had seen it recently?"

"Only to get the appraisal. I gave it back to him," Donald said, but there was a slight quaver in his voice.

"We also found a cache of coins buried near a boulder in the vicinity of the crime scene. The same coins as this one," Dennis continued. "We have those in evidence as well."

Donald's face blanched, but he didn't speak.

"Did you know there were others?" Dennis asked.

"There'd been rumors about them that I heard over the years. My father used to talk about trying to find them."

"I see. Do you know if he ever talked about them to anyone outside the family?"

"No, never!" Donald insisted, his voice regaining its strength. "My father would never have said something if he thought someone else might try to find them."

"Well, alright then. We've been considering the possibility the coins were a motive for the murder." Dennis let that land.

Donald cleared his throat. "I suppose that's possible. Maybe Terry said something about them," he said, brightening at the thought that had come to him to justify a motive that didn't involve him.

Dennis saw Phil nod his head slightly indicating this would be a good place to stop.

"I guess that's all for today, Mr. Dickinson. We'll be in touch if we need anything else."

They all stood to leave.

"I'll walk you out," Phil said, and the two men proceeded down the hall to the main lobby area. Phil returned a few minutes later.

"I think we've got him rattled," he told Dennis.

"Good. Now, we wait and hope he makes a mistake."

CHAPTER TWENTY-ONE

*D*onald walked out of the police station, much less confident about his façade of innocence than when he entered it.

What happened? he asked himself, a little stunned. *Everything was fine, and then...* He replayed the interview, line by line.

It was the question about the appraisal. Maybe you volunteered too much information.

They hadn't said anything, but he remembered the look that had passed between the detectives. *They know something.*

That didn't feel quite right.

They don't know, but they do suspect. If they had any solid proof that I had anything to do with Terry's murder, they would have arrested me. But they let me go.

That restored some of his confidence. He'd reached his car and got inside. His finger was poised above the start engine button when another thought came to him.

But the coins are gone because somehow they found them.

His chest tightened at the realization they were likely gone forever, locked away in evidence until the case was solved. The only way that would happen was if they arrested him and a jury convicted him.

There's no way they can prove it. You burned the branch you hit Terry with. There's no murder weapon, and as long as you keep your cool, they have nothing.

A smile formed at the corner of his mouth. *So what if they've got the coins? I've got the house.*

He started the car and pulled out of the parking lot to return to *his* house.

"Just play it cool and don't slip up," he said aloud, reinforcing the message to himself.

His lips pressed together, and he nodded his head. Certain it was all going to work out in his favor, he hummed along with the song playing on the radio as he drove back to Glen Lake.

CHAPTER TWENTY-TWO

"How are your projects coming along?" Eva asked the group when they were gathered at her dining room table for the next club meeting. "We've only got a little over a week before the festival."

"I've been meaning to thank you for the suggestion about finding fabric with a maple leaf motif, Annalise," Sarah began. "You were right—they had something—so I'm nearly done with the four mug rugs."

"Glad I could help," Annalise replied, smiling.

"My placemats are done," Jennifer announced proudly.

"Leave it to me to make something way more complicated than was necessary. I still have some work to do, but it's nearly finished." Annalise reached down into her project bag and held the wall hanging up for the others to see.

"Oh, Annalise, that is gorgeous! You are such a talented fabric artist," Eva gushed when she saw the piece.

It was a grove of maple trees with buckets hanging from sap taps and in the distance, a maple sugar shack.

The piecing was done, but the free-motion quilting still had sections undone.

"It's not Gregor's sugar shack, but I didn't want to make the design that realistic," Annalise explained.

"I think it's even better making it random—especially considering all the controversy with him this year," Jennifer said.

"I hadn't thought of that when I drew out the design, but you're right," Annalise agreed.

"My table runner is done. I finished hemming the binding this morning," Eva announced.

Sarah cleared her throat, catching everyone's attention.

"I haven't said anything before, but I found something when I was looking through Donald's financials."

"Do Phil and Dennis know about it?" Eva asked when Sarah was finished.

"Yes. They called me after they had an interview with Donald yesterday. He didn't confess, but they didn't expect him to. They just wanted to seed some doubt for now about whether he was a suspect. They think it worked," Sarah said.

"Have you ever encouraged a ghost to haunt somebody?" Annalise asked hesitantly.

Sarah met her eyes, and understanding passed between them.

"No, but this may be a unique situation. I think you're suggesting I get Terry to pull a Caleb Mitchell on Donald."

In the earlier Dylan Johnson case, Caleb Mitchell had tormented his killer, pushing him over the edge until he was ready to confess to the murder. Sarah hadn't been the one to suggest he do it, though.

"Yes," Annalise replied, simply.

Sarah considered the suggestion. "I don't know if it would work—at least not from what Terry has said and how protective he seems to be. He didn't want to implicate Donald and the last time I was with him, he was still holding onto the possibility it could be Gregor."

"Maybe if you told him about the coin I found, and that

Donald had at least one other one to get the appraisal, it would be enough," Jennifer suggested.

"I guess it's possible. It could be he didn't know how many there were—or whether Donald ever found all of them. If Donald lied about what he took, Terry might think everything was accounted for."

"Does this mean we need to take another trip to the grove?" Jennifer asked.

Sarah let out her breath in a deep sigh. "I'd rather not, but if it's what it will take to get Donald to confess, I suppose it's worth it. I'd like to sleep on it before I make a decision, though."

"I get the impression that you're hoping something will happen with Donald so you don't have to," Jennifer teased. "I don't really blame you, though. There's a presence in that grove that gives me the willies."

"Now you know how I feel," Sarah said with a smile.

Reuben jumped up on the chair next to Annalise and swatted at a loose thread in the wall hanging that was dangling over the edge of the table. His claw got stuck in the thread and it slid off the table but Annalise caught it before it fell on the floor.

"Reuben! That's not a cat toy!" Eva reprimanded. "I thought you were over acting like a kitten."

"No harm done, Eva," Annalise reassured her, releasing the thread from his claw.

Reuben shook his paw once Annalise was done and looked at Eva.

I am, but that doesn't mean I can't still have a little fun. It was just hanging there, asking for it to be played with.

Eva didn't know how to respond to that argument.

Besides, it looked to me like this discussion needed to be lightened up. Mission accomplished.

With that, he jumped down and went to the kitchen for a kibble snack.

"He said we needed to lighten up and I think he's right. Time to move on to another topic. How's Liam coming with the commemorative mugs?" Eva asked.

Annalise brightened. "Oh, they are turning out fantastic. I think they're going to be a big hit. He's donating one for the silent auction and a percentage of his profits from the sales of the rest. He said he's made about two dozen so far. Here let me show you."

She scrolled to her Photos file on her phone and passed it around for the others to see.

"That is amazing! If you ask me, he should keep those in his regular stock. Maybe he could even expand into plates or bowls," Jennifer suggested.

"He's way ahead of you," Annalise laughed. "He's got an entire line of pottery planned."

"I can't wait to see it!"

The meeting continued on a lighter note, but in the back of her mind, Sarah was still turning over the idea of convincing Terry to ramp up the pressure on Donald. Jennifer had been right. Sarah hoped the case could be solved without it, but if it couldn't, she'd need to find a way to be okay with whatever decision she made.

CHAPTER TWENTY-THREE

Sarah's last thought before she fell asleep—and her first upon waking—was the same: *should I contact Terry?* She was struggling with a solution for how to move the case forward without crossing a moral line.

She'd taken a break from the day job after finally accepting she wasn't able to concentrate on it and that wasn't going to change by sheer will. Folding laundry wasn't one of her favorite chores, but she was doing it now, hoping it would distract her from her dilemma.

"I must really be desperate if I'm voluntarily doing this instead of working, Max."

Max cocked his head and looked up at her, as though asking her to explain.

"I can't figure out if I should ask Terry to haunt Donald to get him to confess," she explained.

He cocked his head to the other side.

"On the one hand, I want this case to get solved, but on the other hand, I don't feel right about using that method. If he wants to do it on his own, that's one thing but this would be quite another."

Woof, Max agreed.

"Right? I knew you'd agree with me." Sarah's lips turned up in a smile and she gave Max a pat on the head. "Maybe I'll get lucky and Phil and Dennis can solve this one without any more ghost talk from me."

Max woofed again.

She felt a little silly, but talking it out—albeit to a dog—had helped. She realized it wasn't a decision she had to make right now.

"Ashley is going to wish I had more of these predicaments if it means I do extra laundry," she told him as she placed the folded clothes in the basket and carried it upstairs, with Max following on her heels.

After putting away the clothes, she returned to her office, ready to tackle her assignment.

Sarah was deep into her work project when Max's whining broke through her focus. He was looking at a spot near the doorway, but nothing was there. The hair on Sarah's forearms rose.

She felt rather than saw Terry's presence. He wasn't materializing today, but she knew he was there. Before she could speak, an image of Donald popped into her head and she had a sudden emotional reaction.

It wasn't anger. That much she was sure of.

And then the word came—it was disappointment. Its rightness settled within her.

Beneath it was a deep sense of sadness. But both emotions belonged to Terry. There was no doubt in her mind of that.

It lasted only seconds and then he was gone. She shivered when the connection was broken and Max trotted over to her for comforting.

"It's okay, boy. He wasn't here to hurt us." She ruffled his fur and knew her words were as much for herself as they were for Max. "But why did he come to me here?" she murmured.

Several scenarios played in Sarah's head, but none of them

could be answered other than through speculation. She could try to contact Terry for a more definitive answer, but she wasn't ready for that—not yet.

The fact that he'd come to her voluntarily made her think she was building trust with him. He was moving from rejection of Donald's possible involvement to acceptance. It was something she could work with the next time, but it would have to be handled delicately.

Sarah finished her project and stretched her arms over her head, and felt a sense of satisfaction at a job well-done.

"Want to take a ride, Max? I need to go to the grocery store."

He jumped up and brought his leash to her from its hook on the wall.

"I take that as a yes," she said, chuckling.

At the store, she was pushing her cart through the produce section and checking her shopping list when a man brushed by her. Donald didn't know who she was, but she recognized him from pictures she'd seen online.

He stopped to look over the pre-packaged salad selections, giving her time to sneak glances at him. He appeared distracted and there was an air of nervousness about him, as though he was watching for something.

She looked down just before he caught her, but she saw him move away in her peripheral vision. His head swiveled from side to side, but not like he was surveying the grocery aisles.

He's afraid he's being watched, she realized, *and it isn't because of me.*

The detectives were right. They'd rattled him.

CHAPTER TWENTY-FOUR

Sarah didn't see Donald again while she finished her shopping. As soon as she was back in her car with privacy, she called Dennis.

"Hey, Sarah. What's up?" he asked.

"I just saw Donald Dickinson in the grocery store. He's looking very nervous. Whatever you said to him has him looking over his shoulder."

"Interesting. That's just what we were hoping for." Sarah heard the enthusiasm in his tone and was glad she'd decided to call.

"Glad I could help. Have you had any breakthroughs on your end?" she asked.

Sarah winced, wishing she hadn't asked when the enthusiasm left his voice and discouragement came through.

"Not yet. Without finding a weapon, we still don't have anything to tie him to the murder."

"Don't worry—something will turn up. It's happened before." She kept her tone upbeat—maybe too upbeat, she realized. She considered telling him about Terry's visit, but decided against it—knowing it wouldn't change anything.

"That's true," Dennis said. "Hey, thanks for letting us know about seeing Donald. I mean that."

They ended the call and Sarah looked in the rearview mirror. Max was sitting up looking at her and she couldn't help but smile at his happy face in the reflection. Feeling better, she pulled out of the parking space and headed home.

As she drove, the predicament with Terry resurfaced and she accepted that if nothing changed, she might have to contact him after all.

Meanwhile, in Glen Lake, Annalise was in her sitting room preparing for her daily meditation. Soft music was playing, and she lit a stick of Frankincense incense before relaxing in her comfy chair by the window.

She closed her eyes and slowed her breathing, intending only to have a relaxing session before her first client of the day arrived. At first, that's what happened and her shoulders drooped as she settled into a deeper state.

But moments into the meditation, she was jarred out of the pleasant state of relaxation.

She saw a man walking away. He was in a grove of trees and there was snow on the ground. He was stomping his feet as he walked along the path.

Not because of the snow—he's angry, she thought.

There was another emotion there, too—fear of something being withheld—and realized there was a second person on the trail behind him. A sense of righteousness bubbled up and the thought *I'm not giving this up this time* echoed in her head.

She felt a sensation of bending over and saw a man's hand reach out to pick up a section of a branch lying just off the path. Then came a forward motion as the second man approached the one ahead of him.

He raised his arm and then struck the man on the back of the head. The man fell forward, landing face-down in the snow, and then was still.

The attacker stood frozen in place, staring at the motionless body on the ground, and his breath hitched as panic replaced the cold fury he'd felt earlier. He knelt beside the body, fingers pressing against the man's neck. The vision wavered—Annalise felt the surge of panic, the frantic certainty settling in. Whether there was a pulse or not, she couldn't tell. Only that he believed it was over.

The man did a 360-degree turn, looking to see if anyone might have witnessed the scene. Satisfied he was in the clear, he rose and continued onto the path, stomping down the snow to obscure his footprints, still carrying the branch.

When he reached the driveway, he proceeded to another path to the sugar shack located near the house. A wood stove was already lit, and he tossed the branch into it.

The wood hissed and popped when the flames met the snow already melting from the heat.

The man watched until it fully caught and the flames rose higher. Soon all evidence of the weapon would be obliterated, and he smiled—he was in the clear.

The vision ended and Annalise opened her eyes.

"It was Donald," she said softly. "No wonder they haven't found a murder weapon."

She picked up her phone and called the detectives.

"Hi, Annalise. You're the second quilt club lady to call today," Phil told her.

"Oh? Who else called?" she asked.

After he'd told her about Sarah's call and observation of Donald, she said, "You're not going to find a murder weapon."

There was a brief moment of silence on the other end. "What do you mean?" he asked, at last.

She told him about her vision.

"This case just keeps getting better and better," he said sarcastically.

"You might still be able to use this," Annalise suggested.

"You could interrogate him and frame it as a *this-is-what-we-think-happened* scenario. It will have enough of the truth that it might catch him off-guard."

Phil considered her suggestion.

"Maybe…" Phil paused. "He'd have to already be primed so that his emotional state would be unstable to the point he wouldn't counter with logical arguments."

He paused again and Annalise knew he was weighing whether it would work. "He's not ready yet, but he's slipping. With a little more pressure, I think this could put him over the edge."

"He's unraveling, Phil. I truly believe that. Partly because of my intuition, and also from what Sarah saw in the grocery store."

"I hope you're right. No, I believe you're right. You always are," he said, a smile in his voice.

"I've got to go now. A client is coming soon."

"Thanks, Annalise. We appreciate the help," Phil said and disconnected the call.

"We've had a little break," he said to Dennis, who'd only heard half of the conversation. Dennis's eyebrows rose as Phil told him the rest.

"You really think it will work?" he asked Phil.

"Maybe not, but we're running out of options. We've got to at least try—as soon as the time is right."

CHAPTER TWENTY-FIVE

"Ow," Eva exclaimed and stuck her finger in her mouth. She'd already stabbed herself earlier—careless, distracted. That bothered her more than the sting. She prided herself on keeping her hands steady even when her thoughts raced. But not tonight. Lately, everything felt just a little off.

"That's the second time you've stabbed yourself with the needle. Are you okay?" Jim asked.

They were sitting together on the couch in her living room after dinner, watching a movie. Reuben was in his usual spot snuggled between them. He would never admit it, but he'd taken a liking to Jim.

Eva was stitching down the binding on her table runner sans thimble. The movie was one she'd already seen, and she was only half-listening to the dialogue and occasionally glancing up at the screen. On the coffee table, a festival flyer sat beside her sewing basket, its cheerful colors at odds with the knot in her chest.

"I'm fine. Just not paying as much attention as I should with the TV on."

"Didn't you already finish this?" Jim asked, a perplexed expression on his face.

"I finished the one for the silent auction, but I liked it so much I decided to make one for myself."

Jim picked up the tail end of the runner nearest to him to examine it. "This is really nice. How about making another one? I could use a new runner for my dining room table."

Eva narrowed her eyes at him. "Maybe you could just bid on the one at the festival. I think I've had enough practice with this pattern."

"Ouch. Are you sure it's just pricking your finger that has you upset? It seems like you've got something else bothering you."

Reuben lifted his head to look at Eva.

Just say what you're thinking. You don't need to be rude to my friend, he said, flicking the tip of his tail to let her know he wasn't pleased with her attitude.

"All of a sudden you're his wingman?" Eva asked, her voice terse.

Reuben merely stared back at her and she realized she wouldn't be getting any sympathetic support from him.

She huffed out her breath. "Fine." She threaded her needle through the runner to hold it in place. "I can't stop thinking about Donald Dickinson and the festival, and Gregor, and this whole mess. I'd hoped we'd have this wrapped up by now so there wouldn't be any chance of something going wrong during the festival weekend. But now..." She shrugged her shoulders and raised her hands, palms face up.

"Ahhh," Jim said, his tone understanding. "I take it the detectives aren't getting anywhere and neither are any of the ladies?"

"We've had some insights and one possible physical breakthrough, but nothing that's going to get Donald to confess, or enough evidence to arrest him. I just feel so helpless."

"I get it. Not in quite the same way, but there were cases

where we knew the person had to be guilty but couldn't prove it. Sometimes they got away with it. This might be one of those times," Jim offered in an effort to console her, but it had the opposite effect.

There was one case in particular he never talked about. Eva saw it flicker across his face now—the tightening around his eyes, the way his shoulders stiffened. Tonight wasn't the time to ask him to open up about it for several reasons, but the one that was topmost on her mind was her frustration with the Dickinson case.

"That's not good enough. We haven't failed before, and we're not going to this time either," she said with conviction. "I just don't know how yet," she added quietly, the words losing their edge.

"I think people in town are realizing they misjudged Gregor. He was at Checkout when I was picking up some groceries today. I noticed some of the other customers stopping to say hello to him."

"Well, that's good," Eva said, brightening. She was glad she hadn't been one of those who'd shunned him. She wondered how many of them had avoided him just days earlier. How many had quietly—or not so quietly, when he wasn't there to defend himself—decided he was capable of something terrible simply because it was easier than sitting with uncertainty.

"I don't think Gregor's gotten over it completely, though. He spoke to them, but I could tell he wasn't letting his guard down. It will take a while for him to rebuild his trust with them," Jim said.

"Can't say that I blame him. I think I'd be pretty put out if that had happened to me."

"I don't disagree, but it happens a lot. Human nature—the not so pretty side of it—coming out."

"I suppose you're right. I'm sure you must have been a witness to that with your job. It probably has something to do with people wanting to divert attention and have someone to blame to feel safe again."

"That's probably a big part of it," Jim agreed.

"I'm not giving up on Donald being brought to justice, but I do feel better knowing Gregor isn't a pariah in the community anymore," Eva said.

"Good! Maybe now you can finish sewing without poking your finger again," Jim teased.

Amen to that, Reuben mumbled, his voice muffled because his face was tucked down into his front paws.

Eva rubbed his head and back in long, slow strokes, her earlier annoyance forgotten. Reuben stretched out to his full length to take advantage of her attention and his purrs let her know he'd forgiven her.

She removed the needle from the fabric to continue stitching, and this time managed without any more needle jabs. She'd mostly taken Jim's words to heart, but couldn't shake the feeling that she and the other ladies, as well as the detective, needed a break—a big one, and soon. Something disruptive that would knock loose whatever they were all missing.

CHAPTER TWENTY-SIX

The festival grounds were already buzzing with activity when Eva and Jim arrived. The aroma of caramel hung in the air emanating from Gregor's sugar shack.

"Oh, my gosh, I could almost lick the air—it smells so good," Eva said, closing her eyes to fully experience the sensation.

Jim chuckled. "I'm glad you said almost. I might have to pretend I don't know you otherwise."

"Too late. People are already onto us."

"Here come Jennifer and David."

Eva opened her eyes again, and waved to catch their attention. Jennifer returned the wave, and they diverted toward Jim and Eva.

"Good morning. What a beautiful day!" Jennifer exclaimed. "And that smell!" She closed her eyes and inhaled deeply. "I want to take a bite of the air."

Eva poked Jim in the ribs with her elbow. "See? It's not just me."

She explained the reference for Jennifer and David's benefit.

Eva and Jennifer's phones buzzed at the same time.

"It's Annalise. Liam is already here setting up his stall, and she's helping out," Eva said, reading the text. "We should go see if they need any help."

"I was just about to suggest the same thing," Jennifer said, smiling as she tucked her phone back in her pocket. Before she had a chance to do so, it buzzed again, along with Eva's. "Sarah and Ashley are parking their car. I'll let her know they should meet us at Liam's booth."

Jennifer and Eva walked together toward the booths with Jim and David bringing up the rear.

"The festival committee did such a nice job setting everything up," Eva said, admiring the banners hung at the entrance to all the vendor booths which occupied the center of the festival grounds.

"They really went all out this year. I don't remember there being so many booths last year," Jennifer agreed.

There were two rows of booths lined up back-to-back with paths in front of each for prospective customers to peruse the vendors' wares and food offerings, their scents mingling with the maple syrup's.

"I'm so glad they didn't cancel the festival because of Terry's death. I heard Donald decided not to open Terry's sugar shack, though. It was probably too much for him if he had no idea what to do to make the maple syrup," Eva commented.

"He might have a lot else on his mind, too," Jennifer commented wryly.

"There's that."

"I see Annalise," Jim said from behind them. "She's at the end of the row."

As they reached the booth, Sarah and Ashley joined them from the opposite direction.

"Glad you made it," Annalise greeted them. "We're just wrapping up. Doesn't the booth look great?"

Liam came out from the back of the three-sided tent. "Looks

like I'm going to be busy today," he said, surveying the crowd of people.

"This is really something," Sarah said, taking in the arrival of festival attendees queuing up at the booths. "Is it always like this?"

"Jennifer and I were just saying there seem to be more booths this year."

"This is my first time going to a maple syrup weekend event. What should I make sure not to miss?" Ashley asked.

"Make sure to take the tour of Gregor's sugar shack," David suggested. "And get a bottle or two of his syrup. Store-bought is good but his is even better."

"Plus, you'll learn how it's made," Eva added.

"Still the teacher—making sure you get the educational angle in," Jim teased.

"That's okay. I consider myself a lifelong learner," Ashley replied, smiling.

"My kind of person," Eva said. "I'd love to be your first customer, Liam. I've been jonesing for one of your mugs ever since Annalise showed us a picture."

"Come right in. I brought several colors to choose from."

The others walked with them to admire the selections of pottery displayed.

"These bowls are gorgeous!" Ashley exclaimed picking one up to examine it more closely. "I'll wait for Eva to buy her mug, but I'll be your second customer. I want this bowl."

"And I need a new mug, too," Sarah joined in. "What?" she asked, grinning as Ashley arched her eyebrow. "I haven't bought a new mug in ages."

Ashley just shook her head.

"I've been told I have a mug addiction." Sarah explained and looked pointedly at Ashley, but there was no ill will in the gesture—just the amiable banter between couples.

They all made their purchases and Liam offered to keep them while they looked around.

"I'm going to stay to help out, but why don't we meet up later and go for coffee at the Checkout?" Annalise suggested.

"Or you're all welcome to come to our house. We'd have more privacy to talk," Jennifer offered and nodded her head to their left.

The others turned to look and saw Donald on the other side of the festival grounds. He was alone, watchful, looking around as though judging whether it was safe to engage with anyone.

"You're right," Annalise agreed. "That's an even better idea."

"I'll catch up with you," David told Jennifer. "I'm going to go over and say hello. I haven't talked to Donald since the funeral. Maybe this time I can play detective." He gave Jennifer a wink and walked in Donald's direction.

"They went to school together," Jennifer explained to Sarah who was watching his back, a slight frown on her face.

Sarah's face brightened. "That's right. You'd mentioned it before, but I'd forgotten. Has anyone heard from Phil or Dennis with an update?"

Everyone shook their heads.

"I think they're giving him some rope after I called them a couple days ago," Annalise offered. She saw their confused expressions. "Oh, right. I forgot I haven't told you this." She went on to tell them about her discussion with the detectives following her latest vision about the murder.

"That's going to be nearly impossible for them to prove," Jim commented when she was done.

"I think they may get some help," Sarah said cryptically. "I had a visit from Terry."

After Sarah was done recounting Terry's visit, the ladies were silent, thinking about the next move.

Annalise was the first to speak. "I know I encouraged you to get him to put pressure on Donald. Maybe he's coming around to that on his own."

"That's the impression I got," Sarah confirmed.

Sarah noticed Ashley had been quiet during their discussions but was looking uncomfortable

"How about we go check out the sugar shack?" she suggested.

Ashley smiled broadly. "That's a great idea."

"I'll come with you if that's okay," Jennifer offered.

"Of course. The more the merrier," Sarah replied.

"I'd like to look around a little more. I've had more than my share of field trip visits to them when I was a teacher," Eva said.

"You'll be able to find us here when you're done. I can tell we'll be awhile," Jim told them, earning himself a stern look from Eva.

The others wisely departed with a wave and a smile tugging at the corners of their mouths.

A blast of warm air coming out of the stove stack hit them as they got closer to the shack and the caramel scent filled their nostrils even more intensely.

Gregor was inside as a small group of children was gathered around wide-eyed, listening as he explained the process.

"Why don't we look around the shop until this group is done so we can catch his spiel from the beginning?" Jennifer suggested.

"Wow! I was expecting to see just bottles of maple syrup but look at all this stuff!" Ashley said as she saw the displays of maple-flavored products. "And it's not just fudge and candy. Look Sarah, they've got maple mustard, dry rub... Maple-infused tea!"

"That would go great with these apple cider doughnuts with the maple syrup glaze," Sarah said, walking toward the display case where they were stacked. "I think we should definitely get a dozen of these. We can bring them to share at

Jennifer's," she added when Ashley gave her a disapproving look. "Please, mom, I really, really want to try one," she wheedled.

Jennifer laughed. "She's using the mom guilt on you, Ashley. It almost always works with my kids, but not so much with David. Just remember, you're not her mom—only say yes if you want to."

"I hear you," Ashley replied, smiling. "But they really do look good. And as long as we're sharing them with everybody, I can be okay with getting a dozen."

"You heard the woman. Wrap up a dozen for me before she changes her mind," Sarah told the woman behind the counter who had been watching the exchanges with interest and a touch of humor.

"And I'll take a bag of the tea," Ashley said, putting one on the counter.

"That will be yummy in the mug I just bought," Sarah teased.

"You're incorrigible," Ashley said, rolling her eyes.

In the background, they heard snippets of the tour. *It takes forty gallons of sap boiled down to make just one gallon of maple syrup. And you can't rush it. Too much heat and you ruin the whole batch...*

"Did you hear that?" Ashley asked Sarah, her eyes wide. "Is that true?" she asked the woman behind the counter.

"Yup. If that's what Gregor said, you can count on it to be true. He's not a liar."

Jennifer couldn't help thinking about how quickly the residents of the town had doubted his claims of innocence about killing Terry. She knew the woman—Hazel Saucier. She was a lifelong resident of Glen Lake. Jennifer wondered if Hazel had defended Gregor from the beginning. The certainty in Hazel's voice told Jennifer everything, though. Hazel hadn't doubted Gregor—not for a second.

Jennifer placed a jar of the mustard and another of the rub on the counter. "I was nearly out of the rub. David loves it on pork chops. You should try some," she suggested to Ashley and Sarah.

Sarah shrugged when Ashley caught her eye, silently asking if they should. "I'll take a chance on it. I've heard you're a pretty good cook," she told Jennifer.

They were just finishing up paying for their purchases when they heard the announcement that the next presentation would be starting.

"Good timing. If I stayed here any longer, I'd be buying even more stuff I want but don't really need," Ashley said, putting the jar of rub into the bag with the doughnuts and tea.

Ashley and Sarah listened attentively as Gregor explained how the sap was collected in buckets or sometimes with plastic tubing that ran to a central container, then boiled in a pan over a wood fire until the water evaporated or in an evaporator for as long as a full day or more. Once it reached the right temperature and thickened, it was filtered to remove the sugar sand and then bottled while it was hot.

Jennifer had heard the talk many times before and her attention wandered. She was startled to see Donald hovering in a corner at the rear of the room. Their eyes met and held briefly before Donald turned and hurriedly walked out the door. An uneasy feeling came over Jennifer. It was the way he'd looked at her—his eyes cold, but they had a haunted quality to them, too. She was eager to hear how David's conversation had gone with him.

They took their time walking back to Liam's booth, strolling down the lanes where the other vendors were set up. Every now and again, someone would stop Jennifer to say hello. The mood of the crowd was warm and there was an excitement in the air that comes when spring arrives. The feeling of expectation was evident in the way people were greeting each other as though they were ready for a fresh start after a long winter.

"You got here just in time," Eva told them when the group

was together again. "The town manager is about to make an announcement at the main stage."

Groups of people were already gathered at the stage area when they arrived, just as Henry Tillotson climbed the steps to the microphone. A sharp whine of feedback resulted in several people wincing, but when he tried again, the microphone cooperated.

"I want to thank everybody for coming out for the festival. It's great to see so many familiar faces in the crowd. I suspect a few of you have just come out of hibernation."

The crowd laughed at the joke, setting the mood.

"Some of you may be aware that the festival almost didn't happen this year after the tragic death of Terry Dickinson. We're going to miss you Terry and your sense of temper... I mean humor." He paused as the crowd chuckled at his joke.

"Underneath that gruff exterior, we knew there was a kind heart. And a sense of community. If someone needed help, Terry would be one of the first to lend a hand. The town isn't going to be the same without you."

Eva could hear people agreeing with the sentiment throughout the crowd.

"It's been a rough season for some folks recently. I don't have to name names. I think we all know who I mean. Fear makes us quick to judge sometimes—but the town knows how to correct its course and we make amends when we realize we were wrong. I think this community is doing just that."

There was an uncomfortable silence other than the shuffling of feet behind the ladies. Eva caught sight of Gregor standing off to the side, his face expressionless at first and then softening when he heard the town manager's words acknowledging how he'd been treated. Gregor turned to look across the crowd, as if his eyes had been drawn there. What he saw made his jaw set, the muscle twitching before he looked away.

Eva turned in that direction and saw Donald staring back at

Gregor. Whatever was going on between them unsettled her, but the manager was speaking again.

"It's always good to see people return to Glen Lake after time away. No matter what took you away, the town always brings you back."

Eva looked again at Donald who was staring at the town manager. She saw the cold fury in the way he held himself. *That touched a nerve,* she thought.

"And now, we're going to wrap up the festival with the silent auction. I'll turn this over to Olivia Perry, chair of the Maple Syrup Festival Committee."

There was a spattering of applause as Olivia climbed the stairs, a clipboard in her hand.

"Thank you, Henry," she said before turning to face the crowd. "All the bids have been placed and I have our winners. First, let's give a hand for everyone who donated items for the auction. The proceeds are going to go a long way to make next year's festival even better." She paused for the round of applause from the crowd.

She began reading the names of the winners for the various items.

"And now, the winner of the beautiful art quilt made by Annalise Jordan. It brought in a LOT of money, but I'm not surprised. Annalise, it was a museum quality piece if I've ever seen one."

Annalise blushed at the praise and murmured thank you as all eyes turned to her.

"The winner is Liam Campbell."

The crowd began to clap again.

Annalise's mouth dropped open, and she turned to stare at Liam standing beside her. He held up his hands when he thought she was about to protest.

"I didn't bid on it just because you made it. I thought it

would look great on my living room wall. Cross my heart," he said, using his fingers to make the sign.

Her face softened. "Okay. In that case, thanks."

Jim heard raised voices at the edge of the crowd and looked over just as Donald was pushing his way past a man, who was not happy with being moved away so rudely.

On the stage Olivia made her final remarks to close the festival, and the crowd began to disperse.

"We're going to go on ahead so I can get the coffee started," Jennifer told them.

"We won't be far behind. There's a doughnut with my name on it and I can't wait to sink my teeth into it," Sarah announced and then explained for the benefit of those who hadn't witnessed the purchase.

"We'll help you pack up the rest of your things," Eva offered Liam.

"That would be awesome. I don't have much left but they'll need to get wrapped up so they don't break on the way home."

As they were packing, Annalise spoke quietly to Eva. "I'm glad we're meeting at Jennifer's. Did you catch that scene with Donald?"

"I did. I noticed something else but we can talk about it there," Eva replied, keeping her voice soft as well.

"This case may be getting close to the end."

"Let's hope it does before anyone else gets hurt."

She reflected back to the scuffle with Donald. He'd looked dangerous. Not volatile—*focused.* And that, Eva thought, was far more troubling.

CHAPTER TWENTY-SEVEN

"We've got company," Jennifer called out to Matt and Nicky upon arriving home, but there was no response.

"And we brought doughnuts," Sarah shouted.

They heard doors opening and the two teenagers hurried into the kitchen.

"I knew that would get them," Sarah said, giving Jennifer a wink and handed her the bag with the box of doughnuts.

"I wouldn't mind trying some of the tea, if that's okay," Ashley asked.

"Of course! I'll get the kettle on and then start the coffee," Jennifer told her.

"You must be getting excited, Matt. Graduation is almost here," Sarah said.

"Don't remind me," Jennifer groaned. "My little boy is leaving the nest."

"Don't be dramatic, Mom. I'm only going to the Orono campus," Matt said, rolling his eyes. "Besides, I'll probably be home every weekend."

"To have Mom do your laundry," Nicky interjected with a hint of sarcasm.

"Why do you think I picked Orono instead of one of the other campuses?" Matt asked, grinning.

"We'll be happy to have you," David reassured him.

"Besides, I won't be the one doing the laundry," Jennifer stated firmly. "Matt's perfectly capable of doing it himself."

"Sorry, Matt, I didn't mean to get you in trouble," Sarah told him.

"No worries. This is just another day here." Matt grinned. "But to answer your question—yeah, I'm pretty pumped about starting college."

"What are you majoring in?" Ashley asked.

"I'm starting out in Engineering, but we'll see if that's still my major when I graduate."

"There will be no five-year plan unless you pay for the fifth one," David said sternly.

The doorbell rang interrupting the conversation.

"That must be Annalise and Eva. Would you mind getting the door, Dave?"

From the kitchen, they heard the sounds of voices greeting each other and jackets being hung on the coatrack and then footsteps coming up the stairs.

"That didn't take long," Sarah said.

"The extra hands made packing go faster," Liam replied.

"And you'd nearly sold out of everything," Annalise added, looking proudly at Liam.

"Liam, I don't think you've met my kids, Matt and Nicky," Jennifer said, introducing them and they exchanged the traditional *nice to meet you* hellos.

"Why don't we go into the dining room? The kitchen is getting a little crowded," David suggested.

"I'll be right in—the coffee's almost finished. Would you

take these, please?" She handed David a tray with mugs and spoons and gave Nicky a plate stacked with the doughnuts.

A minute later she joined them with the coffee carafe, cream, and sugar and Ashley's tea.

"How is it?" Sarah asked after Ashley had taken a sip.

Ashley paused, thinking about how to describe it. "Interesting," she said at last.

"Maybe it will grow on you," Sarah said, smiling.

"How was the festival?" Nicky asked.

"It was fun," Sarah replied. "Ashley and I had never been to one before. The talk about the process was interesting, and I learned a few things, but I think I liked the gift shop better."

It was Ashley's turn for the eyeroll as she slowly shook her head.

Sarah grinned, but held her tongue.

"Annalise's wall hanging got the highest bid at the silent auction. And well-deserved—it is spectacular," Eva said. "And don't you try minimizing that just because Liam bought it," Eva admonished.

"I second that," Liam said.

"Okay, I give," Annalise said, raising her hands, but she was smiling.

"I'm almost sorry I missed it," Nicky said, but followed it up with "*Almost*. I think I'll need a break for a while after going nearly every year for forever."

"I'll wrap these up for you to take home," Jennifer offered when everyone had finished.

Sarah looked mournfully at the last two doughnuts on the plate. "I'm happy to share, but now I wish I'd bought more. They were delicious!"

"You can have both of them," Ashley reassured her.

"Thanks for sharing," Nicky said, gathering up the empty plates to take into the kitchen.

"I've got a project I need to work on, but thanks, Sarah," Matt said as he lent Nicky a hand.

"Would you please refill the carafe, Nicky? I already have the coffee maker set up," Jennifer asked.

"Sure, Mom."

"Thanks, hon."

Once Nicky returned with the coffee and the teenagers had returned to their rooms, the mood in the dining room turned somber. No one seemed ready to begin the discussion they knew would be heavy. At last, though, Eva took the initiative.

"Did anyone else notice the jabs Henry made in his speech?" Eva asked.

"I sure did," Jennifer replied. "I was surprised he said it out loud, but I think the people who had treated Gregor badly got the point."

"It didn't go over Donald's head either. I saw Gregor and him giving each other the evil eye," Eva said.

Jennifer refilled her mug and passed the carafe on to the others.

"When we were in the gift shop, Hazel Saucier came to Gregor's defense. She said he wasn't a liar. We weren't even talking about the murder, but I got what she was really talking about," Jennifer told them.

"I saw Donald in the back of Gregor's shack while Sarah and Ashley were listening to his talk. We made eye contact, and he left like he had something to hide and he didn't want to be seen," she continued.

"And then when Henry made that comment about people coming back," Eva said. "I happened to look over at Donald."

She shivered slightly.

"It got to Donald. He looked like he could spit. He really took it personally," she said.

The group was quiet as they took in what Jennifer and Eva had shared.

"You haven't told me how it went when you talked to Donald," Jennifer reminded David.

"You may already know this, but Donald and I went to school together, so I thought it would be a nice gesture to say hello. He was standing off by himself. I'd thought he was just feeling awkward about approaching anyone, but after what you just said, I'm not so sure."

"I agree. It sounds like he's purposely avoiding people," Jim said.

"So, was he okay with you talking to him?" Jennifer asked.

"He was polite about it, but it felt forced. And he kept it to the bare minimum. I asked him how he was doing after Terry's death and all he said was *things have a way of working out*."

David struggled for the right words.

"He didn't seem like it had phased him at all. There was something else, though. Not anger or grief. He seemed... finished. Like he's already past it. I know they weren't really close, but it still seemed off to me."

"Like he didn't really care?" Annalise asked.

"There was a bit of that. And maybe like he wasn't sorry that Terry was dead."

"I don't think he is," Annalise replied.

She told them about her vision and certainty that it was Donald who had committed the murder.

"The impression I was left with matches what you said, David. At first he was shocked, but it wasn't so much about having killed Terry. It was a *what do I do now* kind of feeling. And then almost immediately, he switched to getting rid of the evidence and going on as though nothing happened."

"Do Phil and Dennis know?" Eva asked.

"Yes, but they can't use it to arrest him, so they're keeping the information in their back pockets."

"When Terry came to me a few days ago..." Sarah began.

"Wait a minute. Back up the bus," Annalise cut in. "Terry came to *you*?"

Sarah smacked her forehead lightly. "Sorry, I've been busy with work and forgot to tell you all. He didn't say anything, so I didn't actually talk to him. But I was aware of his emotional state."

"You'd think I'd be used to this by now," David teased. "But it still surprises me. Sorry, didn't mean to interrupt."

"I know exactly how you feel," Ashley commiserated, making everyone smile.

"Anyway," Sarah continued. "I'm sure he knows it was Donald. What I felt was disappointment. I don't think I'm going to have to ask him to haunt Donald. I think it's already happening, and that has a lot to do with how he's acting now."

"After the way he left the festival and pushed that guy out of the way, I got a very bad feeling. I think he may be getting dangerous—like an animal who's been cornered," Eva said.

The air in the room became heavy with the weight of her words.

"Should you tell the detectives about all of this?" Ashley asked.

It was a reasonable question, and the ladies considered.

Jennifer was the first to speak. "I don't think so. There's nothing new to tell them that would be useful."

"I agree," Sarah said. "They know what Annalise and I experienced, but it doesn't change the facts they have to work with."

They sat with that for a moment.

"Well, we should probably get going, Jim," Eva said. "Thanks for having us over Jennifer. And thanks for sharing, Sarah. I could have eaten another one, but I didn't want my hand slapped," she teased.

"Never," Sarah assured her, but paused for dramatic effect. "Well, maybe never. They are pretty good."

That was followed with laughter from everyone.

"We should get going, too. Max probably needs to go outside," Ashley reminded Sarah.

"And us," Annalise said, standing, and Liam stood, too.

Once they were in the car, Eva reflected on the day's events. Whatever Donald was planning, after seeing his behavior and hearing the others' encounters with him, Eva was certain that Donald was still orchestrating events.

Terry's murder had been an act of impulse, but Donald's emotional state that preceded it, continued to shape his reactions. He was careful, meticulous in his planning.

And the most dangerous thing of all was that Donald believed he was still in control.

CHAPTER TWENTY-EIGHT

*D*onald slammed the front door behind him and threw his jacket onto a chair.

"Why did I think I could come back to Glen Lake? Even when he's dead, Terry is still the golden boy."

Eva's assumption was correct—Henry Tillotson's tribute to Terry and not-so-subtle reference to Donald's return had touched a nerve.

"What a load of sanctimonious garbage," he continued to rage.

Don't let it get to you, his inner voice reassured him. *What they think of you means nothing. You made something of yourself when you left here. You don't need their approval.*

That calmed him.

It was true, he was a success at his job and his father didn't matter anymore—he was dead. Just like Terry. He couldn't get their approval now even if he did want it.

Put it behind you and get on with your life.

While he was waiting for the kettle to boil for a cup of tea, he went into the butler's pantry. It was better than when he'd arrived, but still cluttered. Terry had been a slob—Donald was a neatnik.

Donald had already filled two trash bags with cans of food that had long passed their expiration dates. Putting things back in order wasn't just about being tidy. It gave him control and put his stamp on the house. *This is mine now and I'm going to erase all traces of you, Terry.*

The tea kettle whistled loudly, and he returned to the main portion of the kitchen. He'd get back to the de-cluttering later. He took his mug of tea into the living room, intending to pick up where he'd left off reading the book he'd brought with him.

It was something else that set him apart from his father and brother. Donald loved to read. He'd be surprised if they ever picked up a book once they were no longer in school. It gave Donald a sense of superiority over them.

He was immersed in the book when a memory jerked him out of his concentration.

You can pretend you're better than me till the cows come home. The house is still mine and you'll never get your hands on it.

Terry had told Donald that after they'd left the attorney's office for the reading of his father's Will. He could still see the smug, satisfied expression on Terry's face.

"Guess you were wrong about that, weren't you bro?" Donald said aloud.

Was I?

The thought had popped into his head as though Terry was there in the room with him, but Donald knew better. Terry wasn't haunting him, but his obnoxious personality was still interfering.

"You never knew when to stop, did you? You always had to get the last word."

He spoke the words bitterly. There was no relief in hearing them or knowing that Terry hadn't actually spoken them. It was Donald's past that was haunting him.

"I did what I had to do. I had no other choice. It's time to put this to rest and get on with my life. I'm the one in control—remember that."

CHAPTER TWENTY-NINE

"I've got to be missing something, Max."

Sarah reached down absently to stroke his head. On her desktop, the folder for Donald Dickinson was open displaying the various files she'd gathered. She'd been through them several times but still nothing had jumped out at her other than the appraisal for the coin.

It was mid-morning and her coffee had gotten cold. She went to the kitchen for a fresh cup and saw the last doughnut from the festival in a glass storage bowl sitting on the counter.

"That's coming with me!"

Sarah returned to her office and took a bite of the doughnut savoring the rich maple glaze blending with the apple and spices of the cake portion. She washed it down with a sip of coffee before returning to her task.

"Okay, let's look at this logically. We need to get into Donald's head."

Woof, Max agreed.

"Donald is a control freak. He rarely uses his credit or debit cards which means he prefers cash. That says to me he doesn't want to leave digital trails."

Living his life like that had stymied her and the detectives in finding anything out of the ordinary to look into further.

"The appraisal was a mistake, but he probably didn't think anyone would find it... Or maybe he meant to delete the email, but forgot."

That didn't quite jibe as she considered it.

"Nope, I think he was so sure of himself that it never occurred to him to delete it. So, what else might he have kept that matters here?"

She thought about how he'd been able to cover his tracks, blocking any way to catch him up. The wall clock's tick tocks were the only sounds as she played over his explanations for his whereabouts on the day of Terry's death.

"Am I projecting there's anything suspicious based on my emotions after my interactions with Terry?" The doubt crept in, but she pushed on, determined to make the case logically, not just emotionally.

Phil and Dennis had told her Donald said he was driving to Glen Lake for a planned visit with Terry. He arrived after the murder and the timeline fit the time it would have taken him to arrive from his home in southern Maine.

"But we know he was already there, don't we, Max?" She reassessed her earlier doubts and felt a certainty in her gut that she hadn't been wrong. "Terry didn't come out and admit it, but *we* know he knew."

Max whined softly—perhaps remembering Terry's unexpected, and unwelcome for Max, visit to their house.

"So that means he had to have left after he killed Terry, burned the branch, and then came back in time for Deputy Tremblay to do the notification. So where was he?"

Sarah considered various scenarios, making notes on a pad of paper. She dismissed the possibility he'd just driven around waiting for the police to show up. He'd already been driving for over two hours just to get to Glen Lake.

What would I do if I needed to kill some time?

She took another bite of the doughnut, licking the glaze off her fingers, and then pressed her finger into the crumbs still on the plate before popping it into her mouth, when a thought occurred to her.

"If it was me, I'd go get something to eat."

That felt right, but she cautioned herself. *If I'm wrong about this, everything collapses.*

"He'd want to use cash. He's smart enough to know if he used his debit or credit card, there'd be a record of where he ate. Maybe not the time, but definitely the date and the place which means the detectives could always ask if anyone saw him."

She was ready to move on to another possibility, but stopped when she realized he might have needed to take out cash at an ATM. It was a long shot but maybe he was set up to get text or email notifications if he took out a certain amount.

Checking that would mean accessing his emails again. It wasn't something she was entirely comfortable with, but as before, she reminded herself it might be the only way to find something that could trip him up. But there could be consequences—serious ones—for her if her intrusion was discovered.

"You're not being nosy or trying to get into his account," she said, needing the pep talk.

"You're just looking for any clue to prove he was already here. Just make sure you do it right and cover your tracks."

She looked down at Max who met her gaze. "Let's hope he didn't learn his lesson after the appraisal and delete anything."

Taking a deep breath, she accessed his emails again and scanned through the emails to the date of Terry's murder and let out a *whoop,* raising both fists in the air, when she saw the bank alert.

Sarah hesitated before opening the email, her anxiety about being discovered returning. She double-checked that she'd done this invisibly and confident she had, clicked on the message.

She'd been holding her breath again, and let it out slowly. Relief flowed through her when she read the information confirming he'd taken out the cash at a Bangor branch and the time of the withdrawal confirmed it would have been when he claimed to still be on his way to Glen Lake.

"Okay, that's step one. Phil and Dennis will have to get a warrant to search his bank records, but what else could they do to find out where he was all that time?"

After a few minutes of brainstorming, all her time spent watching forensic and police procedural shows kicked in.

"They could triangulate his phone! It wouldn't give them the exact location, but it would narrow it down."

She deliberated her next step. The only logical one was to turn this over to the detectives. They would have to get the warrant to prove what she'd found.

"Sarah Pascal," Phil said, his voice upbeat. "What good news do you have for me today?"

"I'm hoping it will be more than just a theory."

She was reluctant to spoil his upbeat mood, but she also didn't want to give him false hope either. What she was about to ask him to do wouldn't be easy.

She explained how she'd had the idea to check Donald's emails for a bank alert and found one that proved he was already in Bangor. Then she asked if they'd looked into his phone whereabouts.

"That's a great find, Sarah," Phil said, his tone cautious. "We'll have to convince a judge to get a warrant, but I think we can make the case for both the ATM withdrawal and his phone records. We want to make sure we do this right."

"Of course. Donald's been able to get around where he was so far, but maybe this will be enough to wear him down and he'll slip up."

"Let's hope you're right. I'm going to get on this now. We'll let you know how it goes."

Sarah turned to face Max and ruffled the fur under his chin with both hands.

"Cross your paws, Max. This may be our big break."

He jumped up barking several times, his tail wagging, making his entire back end sway from side to side.

Sarah couldn't help but laugh, but sobered again when she realized how much depended on everything having to fall into place. She'd done her part. It was all she could do for now.

CHAPTER THIRTY

It had been several days since the festival. Donald had mostly put it behind him, in large part by immersing himself in the pantry decluttering. He was nearly at the end of sorting out all the expired items. To his disgust, he'd even found a few cans of beans that dated back to before his father died. His father had always insisted they might "come in handy someday," as if scarcity were just around the corner. Donald dropped them into the discard box harder than necessary, the metallic clatter echoing his irritation.

Once it was completely cleaned out, he planned to paint. Painting would be putting another stamp on its ownership being his even though he'd decided to sell the house. It would be the final erasure of his father and brother—his entire family history, for that matter. Refreshing the rooms with a coat of paint would help the resale. Perhaps not monetarily, but possibly how long it would stay on the market. The sooner he could get this part of his life behind him, the better.

He was on the ladder removing items from the top shelf when the doorbell rang. He wasn't expecting anyone—he had no friends or family who would visit.

Probably another real estate agent wanting me to list the property with them, he thought and ignored the bell. Less than a minute later, it rang again—twice, this time. He considered ignoring that one as well, but it rang a third time. The insistence irritated him. Whoever it was, clearly didn't understand boundaries—or didn't care about them.

Letting out an exasperated sigh, he climbed down the ladder and went to the front door. Through the sidelight, he saw two men in suits standing on the porch.

They don't look like real estate agents. And then he recognized them—the detectives investigating Terry's death. He felt a brief tightness in his chest, but only for a second. *Nothing to worry about. If they had anything concrete, they wouldn't be standing on his porch asking politely.*

He opened the door and their neutral expressions confirmed his assessment.

Then why are they here? His brain didn't have time to dwell on that thought as the taller one—*Detective Robertson?*—spoke and ended Donald's internal dialogue.

"Good afternoon, Mr. Dickinson. Sorry to bother you without calling ahead, but we won't take much of your time. Do you mind if we come in?"

Do I have a choice? Donald thought, but instead said, "Not at all. I was organizing the pantry. Nothing that couldn't wait."

He stepped aside so the detectives could enter and gestured to the living room on the left.

"Can I offer you coffee? It wouldn't take long."

It was the polite thing to do, but he hoped they wouldn't accept. They'd tried to trip him up the last time and he would have to be more careful. Getting them out of the house quickly was the best option.

"No, thank you. As I said, this shouldn't take long," Detective Robertson said, sitting beside his partner on the couch opposite Donald.

They chose the couch without asking—his couch—and the small presumption needled him more than it should have.

Donald's compulsive neatness was triggered when he saw the dust motes in the shaft of sunlight above the detective's head, momentarily distracting him, and made a mental note to vacuum and dust the room later.

The one Donald remembered as Detective Smith took a notebook from his jacket pocket and flipped through the pages to find his notes.

"I assume you're not any closer to finding who killed my brother?"

"We have someone in mind, but that's all we can tell you for now."

Donald forced himself to remain composed. *You already know if they had anything solid, they'd be here with an arrest warrant.*

"We're revisiting a few details about everyone's movements the day of the murder. We just want to make sure we have your morning right. Would you tell us what happened from the time you left your house until your arrival here at your brother's house?" Smith asked.

Donald stuffed down his annoyance at the detective's use of the word murder and referring to the house as his brother's. It wasn't a murder, and this was *his* house now.

"I left my house at about nine."

His mind was racing—*was that the time he'd told them before?* The answer hovered just out of reach, and he hated that uncertainty. He forced himself to keep his expression neutral.

Dennis looked at his notes again.

"Deputy Tremblay's report says you arrived at noon. Did you stop along the way?"

"I hadn't had breakfast, and was getting hungry but I didn't want to impose on my brother, so I went to get some lunch."

"Where was that?" Dennis asked.

"At Denny's—the one at the mall."

The detective wrote that down in his notepad.

"Do you recall what time you arrived?"

"Not exactly, but I would guess it had to be around eleven, given the time I left my house. It only takes about two hours to drive here." He added the detail automatically, the way people did when they wanted their answers to sound logical.

Smith made another notation.

"And you didn't stop anywhere else?"

The question was harmless on the surface, but Donald felt a sense of unease worming its way into his consciousness.

"No." He kept his voice steady. They didn't need to know about the ATM.

The detectives exchanged a brief look—subtle, but Donald noticed. He considered if it held any deeper meaning, but their demeanor didn't indicate anything for him to be concerned about. Still—the entire line of questioning seemed like more than just double-checking his whereabouts.

Donald heard Terry's disapproving voice from long ago in his head. *You're going to have to learn to lie better than this, brother. You may be book smart, but you're not street smart.*

Terry had always said it with a smirk, like it was a joke. It never had been. A scowl appeared on his face before he could stop it. He'd heard Terry tell him that his entire life and the feeling of being judged grated on Donald. Smith was looking at his spiral notepad and didn't notice, but Robertson did. Donald could see it in the way he was studying him.

Detective Smith closed his notebook and returned it to his pocket. "That should do it for now."

The men rose to leave and Donald's shoulders relaxed.

"Thank you for your time. We'll be in touch if anything else comes up," Robertson said.

Donald didn't immediately return to the pantry. He replayed the scene in his mind, chastising himself for not making notes for himself about what he'd told them previously. They'd tricked him again into telling them where he was. They could check that.

He walked back to the pantry, but something had changed. It had a claustrophobic feel to it now, like the walls were closing in, crowding out the sense of order he'd been so careful to restore.

The tightness in his chest returned, stronger this time—and it didn't go away.

~

"HE LOOKED MORE NERVOUS THIS TIME," Phil commented when they were back in the car.

"He did, didn't he?" Dennis replied, a satisfied smile on his face.

"The warrant should be coming through soon. Let's hope he's still shaken when we bring him in to grill him about the ATM receipt time stamp."

"In the meantime, I'm feeling hungry. Let's grab a bite. We haven't been to Denny's in a while," Dennis said.

"I was just about to suggest the very same thing."

CHAPTER THIRTY-ONE

The next meeting of the quilt club was a social gathering. They hadn't picked a new project for the next month, and no one brought it up. It was as though everyone knew that even though the festival was over, there was still too much unfinished business to move on just yet.

Eva had suggested they all bring scraps from their fabric stashes to organize. They each had a section of the eight-foot cutting table and a bin of scraps from their collections.

"When I first joined the club, I had hardly any fabric at all. And I didn't think I'd ever have a supply like yours, Eva," Sarah said as she dumped her bin onto the table.

"It's still a long way from catching up and I don't think I ever will, but I can't believe how quickly it's adding up."

The other ladies chuckled. They'd been quilting for decades and they had multiple bins to sort.

"What should I do with all this?" Sarah asked, spreading out the material.

"Here's how I tackle mine," Eva began. "First take the biggest scraps and decide if you want to keep them as is or cut them down into smaller standard sizes that you can have on hand. They're great for making scrappy quilts."

"What about these smaller ones?" Sarah asked.

"If they need it, I iron mine first to make it easier to cut," Annalise suggested. "Sometimes I use some starch when I iron."

"That's a good tip, Annalise," Eva complimented. "Depending on how big—or small—they are, I cut mine into five-inch, two-and-a-half-inch, or two-inch squares. If they're smaller than that or odd shapes, I put them into my bin for crumb quilts."

"Gotcha. That makes sense."

"I'm a gadget girl so I've got rulers that can help that go quicker if you want to borrow them," Eva offered.

"Of course you do," Sarah teased, "but thanks, I'd like that."

The room became quiet except for the sound of rotary blades slicing through fabric as they each fell into a rhythm of cutting and sorting their pieces.

"This is actually pretty meditative," Sarah remarked after a while.

"And I always feel so accomplished once I've got my stacks of squares piled up and my bin is empty," Jennifer said. "It makes me want to find a scrappy project to use them up."

"Me, too," Annalise said, smiling at Jennifer.

"Actually," Jennifer said slowly, "this does give me an idea. I've been thinking about making Matt a quilt for his dorm room. A scrappy quilt would be perfect for that."

"You're welcome to take a look through my pattern books to see if there's one you like," Eva offered.

"Thanks, Eva." Jennifer wandered over to the bookcase with several shelves lined with various quilting books and browsed through the titles before selecting two.

"You haven't said anything about the detectives getting a warrant to access Donald's bank account and phone records. I'm guessing that means it's still waiting for approval?" Annalise asked Sarah.

"As far as I know, they haven't got it yet. They did tell me they went to Donald's house and questioned him again about his whereabouts. He didn't break, but the guys said they thought there was a crack by the time they left."

"I sure hope they can get it settled soon. I hate this feeling of being on pins and needles waiting for it to be wrapped up," Eva said.

"I know what you mean," Annalise said. "The waiting when you know what should happen makes it even worse."

"I'd thought that Henry's speech at the festival might be enough to put Gregor's guilt to rest, but there are still some hold-outs," Jennifer said, looking up from the quilt book.

"Not everyone heard it," Eva reminded her, "but you're right. I'm surprised the gossip mill didn't spread the word."

"Yet another reason why I wish Donald could be arrested and confess. That would stop it," Annalise said.

No one disagreed—but no one looked entirely comfortable with how much damage had already been done.

Sarah had remained quiet during the discussion, lost in her own thoughts about the situation. She'd learned that sometimes saying nothing was the only way to listen properly. When it seemed like it was the proper moment to move on, she said, "I'd hoped that I was right about Terry intervening on his own. If he is, he's taking his sweet time about it."

"He hasn't been back?" Eva asked.

"No, but I don't think he's entirely gone. I'm not sure how to describe it. Sometimes I feel a presence almost as though they're right there in the room with me. Other times, it's like an echo. No, that's not quite right."

She thought for a moment to find the right words.

"This probably sounds weird, but it's like they're slippery. I can't quite keep my hold on them but I know they're there." She paused, still not satisfied with her explanation, and then brightened as an idea came to her. "It's like a radio station you try to tune in, but the signal isn't strong enough. I guess that's a better way to put it. That's Terry. His signal is weak."

"Do you think he's ready to cross over?" Annalise asked.

Sarah didn't hesitate. "I don't get that impression at all—not yet."

The room fell quiet again until Jennifer exclaimed, "This one is perfect! I think Matt would love it." She brought the book over to share with the others.

"I think it's got just the right touch of masculine and grown-up. I have to keep reminding myself that he's almost an adult," her voice trailed off.

The others couldn't personally share in her feelings since none of them had children of their own, but they understood what she must be going through.

Sarah's phone beeped, and they waited as she read the text.

She looked up from her phone; surprise and relief flickered across her face.

"They got the warrant. They're on their way to pick up Donald now."

There was a collective sigh of relief, but they each knew it wasn't the end. Donald would still have to confess. But at least now they were finally one step closer.

CHAPTER THIRTY-TWO

It was another day after the warrants arrived before the detectives had the information they needed to arrest Donald. The ATM receipt and phone triangulation put him in Bangor and at Terry's house at the time of the murder, not several hours later as he'd claimed.

"We've got him," Phil said with a sense of satisfaction. "Let's go pick him up and finish this."

They arrived at Donald's house with the arrest warrant in hand a half hour later.

Donald's expression when he answered the door was its usual—neutral, controlled, with a bit of arrogance underneath. But his eyes had a haunted look about them, and he didn't seem surprised to see the detectives standing on his doorstep.

"Mr. Dickinson, we're here with a warrant for your arrest," Dennis began and read Donald his Miranda rights.

They'd expected some pushback but there was none.

"Fine. Let's get this over with so I can get back to my projects. You're going to be regretting you wasted your time focusing on me."

"We won't need to be cuffing you, will we?" Phil asked.

Donald glared at him. "I'm not some common violent criminal. Of course you won't need to handcuff me."

They placed him in the back of their car and returned to the police station. After he was booked, he was returned to an interrogation room where Phil and Dennis were waiting. Donald had declined a call to an attorney claiming he wasn't guilty and didn't need one.

Donald sat stone-faced opposite them, his eyes cold with fury. The room was bright, the furniture institutional, and he felt cold, despite the actual temperature being sixty-nine degrees. He was still in denial that this would result in anything other than his release and the charges being dropped. They had no proof he'd been at Terry's house and, what he felt was even more important —no murder weapon.

They began with the preliminaries—informing him the interview would be recorded, then reading the information about the case once the recording began.

"Just get it over with so I can get out of here," Donald said, still convinced that would be the ultimate outcome.

He answered their questions smoothly—just as he'd rehearsed them in his head. It didn't hurt to be prepared just in case the unthinkable happened. Their second visit had prompted him to do so. Everything was going as he expected and his annoyance ratcheted up until they brought out their bombshell.

"We found a discrepancy about the time you arrived," Phil told him, holding his gaze. He opened the file folder on the table in front of him and took out what looked like a typed report.

Donald's breath hitched and his shoulders tensed. *How did they find out? I must have told them the wrong time the second time they questioned me.*

"According to your bank's records..."

"You can't look through my bank records," Donald voice was indignant.

"We had a warrant, Mr. Dickinson," Phil replied calmly.

Donald started to protest again, but closed his mouth, his lips disappearing into a thin line.

"According to your bank's records," Phil began again. "you withdrew cash at an ATM on Broadway in Bangor at approximately seven AM. Your cell phone pinged in Glen Lake fifteen minutes later. That's at least five hours before you claimed to have arrived. Would you care to explain that?"

Donald felt both detectives' eyes on him and his confidence began to slip away.

"It must be a mistake. I did stop at an ATM, but it was just before I went to Denny's. That was at around eleven, not seven."

"It's no mistake, Mr. Dickinson. And your phone carrier verifies the time in the same window as the bank withdrawal. They can't both be wrong—or both be the wrong hour."

Donald swallowed hard and his mind raced. He might need to change tactics. He could still talk his way out of this.

"All right, I admit I came earlier than I said before. I wanted to get the rest of the coins before Terry saw me. The only way I could do that was to get there early enough that there would be daylight but before he was up and about. But when I got there, he was already up, so I left."

"Where did you go for the five hours before you came back?"

Donald's confidence returned because he had an explanation that would put him in the clear.

"I was going to drive back to my house, but when I drove past the motels by the airport, I got the idea to rent a room and try again the next morning."

"We didn't find any charges on your credit card for a motel room," Dennis said.

"I paid cash. I already had the money from the ATM." His tone was smug when he gave them the name of the motel. Even if they checked with the motel, it would be confirmed. He was in the clear.

This was just the information they needed but hadn't been able to ask before without revealing they knew about Donald's earlier arrival. "We'll need a moment to confirm that," Dennis told him.

"You do that," Donald replied, a self-assured look on his face.

They stepped out of the room into the hallway.

"You go check to see if they had a room paid for in cash that day around that time," Phil said. "I'll wait here and think about how to push him when you get back."

Dennis returned a few minutes later. "He was telling the truth. The motel had a check-in form with his name, time and room number, along with his license plate number. And I talked to the clerk who was on duty that day. He remembered him.

"That's actually good news. It confirms he was here. I think we can still do this using Annalise's vision. If we lay it out like we already know—every step, every motive—he won't be able to keep pretending he's smarter than us.

When he was done, Dennis smiled. "Let's do this."

Dennis began, acting as though the motel room had made everything okay.

"The motel verified your stay and that you'd paid with cash. It's not easy these days to find a motel that will do that without a credit card, but you picked the one that would."

Donald gave him a look of disgust that his integrity had been questioned.

"That explains where you were, but if you didn't plan to come back until the next day, why did you show up later that day?"

"I had time to think and wanted to talk it out with Terry—convince him the coins weren't worth that much and I was the one who'd discovered them in the first place. He should just let me have them."

"That seems reasonable," Phil said, nodding his head as

though he completely understood and agreed with Donald's thinking.

Donald relaxed. *It had worked. He'd be out of here in no time.*

"Here's what we think really happened," Dennis began and then went on to describe Annalise's vision. As he did, Donald's face blanched and his eyes flickered.

"That's a nice theory," he said, but his voice was hesitant.

"Is it?" Phil questioned.

They've got you, brother. I told you that you needed to learn how to lie better. Just like always, you're a loser.

Donald jerked when he heard Terry's voice in his head. It wasn't like before when they were memories from his youth. This sounded external, as though Terry was right there with him. Donald's head swiveled scanning the room, looking for the source of Terry's voice, but there was no one else there.

Time to 'fess up.

"You wouldn't listen. All you had to do was give me the coins." He spoke to the empty spaces in the room as the detectives exchanged glances. Phil's idea was working.

Donald turned to the detectives.

"I didn't mean for it to go that far but I had no choice."

There was no apology in the confession. No hint that he felt he'd done anything wrong.

"I had no choice," Donald repeated.

His shoulders drooped and at first he felt a sense of relief that he wouldn't have to keep up the charade and surely they understood. But then, he was enveloped with a feeling of emptiness as he realized he'd sealed his fate. The satisfaction he'd expected by removing Terry from his life had been temporary.

The silence in the room weighed on all of them.

"I think we're done. An officer will take you back to your cell." Phil closed the folder and shut off the recording.

Donald slumped in his chair, his defeat complete.

The detectives watched his back as the officer led him back to lock up.

"You did it," Dennis said, congratulating Phil.

"Maybe. But I had the sense we had some help."

"I had the same feeling," Dennis admitted. "Either way, it doesn't really matter. We wanted a confession, and that's what we got."

Phil clapped Dennis on the shoulder. "Come on, let's get our report written and make it official. Then we celebrate."

Dennis grinned. "I'll even pick up the tab."

CHAPTER THIRTY-THREE

$\mathcal{B}$efore going out to celebrate, the detectives called Gregor as a professional courtesy.

"Mr. MacHenry, we have some news we'd like to share. We've arrested Donald Dickinson for the murder of his brother, Terry, and he's confessed," Dennis told him.

"I'm sorry. Did you say Donald Dickinson killed him?" Gregor asked, not quite believing he'd heard correctly.

"That's right. He confessed and gave a full statement about what happened that day."

Gregor didn't know what to make of the news and paused to absorb it before replying.

"Thank you. Thank you for letting me know—and for believing me when no one else did. I know I was the prime suspect, but you didn't stop looking for someone else when you could have. I appreciate that more than you know."

"We wouldn't have been doing our jobs if we'd taken the easy way. You deserved better than that."

Gregor hung up the phone, still feeling numb by the news. It hadn't shocked him that the brothers were at odds—they always had been. What stunned him was that Donald would have been the one to take it to that extreme. He'd always been the quiet one, in control of his feelings. Terry was the one with the volatile temper.

They'd always fought. I just never thought one of them would go so far as to kill the other one because of it.

Gregor grabbed his jacket. He needed to get outside, into the daylight to shake the heaviness that had overcome him.

He walked toward the maple grove. The snow had completely melted, but the ground was still damp and muddy as the remaining frost below the surface thawed. There was more bird activity now. The year-round chickadee residents were joined by more recent arrivals of red-winged blackbirds and robins and their calls broke the silence of the woods, along with the chattering of squirrels.

As he walked, Gregor thought about his quarrel with Terry. There was a sense of reprieve that it hadn't been what led to Terry's death, but he also couldn't help think about what a waste it had been. Had a dispute about three maple trees been worth it —or was that how every man justified himself before crossing a line?

He'd reached the spot where he'd found Terry and stopped.

It had been a different argument that ended in his death, but were the circumstances lying beneath the surface that much different? Both he and Donald had been fighting for what they thought of as principles. That mattered. But weren't principles supposed to support their humanity, not destroy it?

"I'm sorry it ended like this for you, Terry. You were a cantankerous person to be around sometimes—a lot of the time, if we're being honest. But in your own way, you were a decent human being. You deserved to live out your natural life."

Gregor stood for a moment, then felt something loosen in his chest. He didn't question it. He turned back toward the house lighter than when he'd arrived.

Later that day, he went to the Checkout for dinner—less a celebration than an attempt to feel normal again.

The diner was nearly full and the only open seat was at the counter. That suited Gregor just fine. He could sit by himself and not feel the need to speak to anyone. When he entered the room, he felt several sets of eyes on him and an air of awkwardness in the room.

People squirmed in their seats and their eyes darted back to their meals, avoiding any eye contact with Gregor.

Nothing's changed, he thought, with a mixture of resentment and sadness.

Betty approached him, coffee carafe in hand.

"Evenin' Gregor. I heard the news about Donald Dickinson being arrested for Terry's murder." Her voice was intentionally raised to carry through the room. "I never thought you were guilty but now there are a lot of people in this town who owe you an apology."

She looked around the room, purposely resting on those she was directing her message to. They immediately looked away, their faces reddening.

"Thanks, Betty. That means a lot to me." Gregor's voice was sincere and his expression held a deep appreciation for what she'd said—and that she'd intended it for everyone there.

"You're most welcome. Now, what can I get you?"

Gregor ate his meal in silence, but slowly diners approached him, testing his reaction to their presence, and offered their apologies which he accepted graciously. Somehow, though, the apologies didn't carry the weight he thought they would. Their words felt hollow and inside, the hurt remained that they would have thought so little of him in the first place.

They might be moving on, but it would take longer before he would be able to trust them again. He wasn't shutting down the chances of it happening, but he respected that he needed to feel his feelings first and process them.

Betty brought his check and a piece of his favorite pie. "On the house," she said, giving him a smile and a wink.

It helped. Not everyone had convicted him in the court of public opinion and for now, they were the ones who would help him move on.

CHAPTER THIRTY-FOUR

*M*ax's low whine pulled Sarah's attention from the computer screen. She frowned at him at first, unsure what had unsettled him, then felt it—the subtle shift in the room that had nothing to do with sound or movement.

"It's okay, Max," she murmured.

He crossed the room and pressed against her legs, his weight solid and reassuring. Sarah rested a hand on his back and took a slow breath. The house was otherwise unchanged. The faint hum of the refrigerator downstairs. The steady tick of the clock on the wall. The cursor on her screen blinked patiently, waiting.

Sarah knew who it was.

Since hearing about Donald's arrest, she'd sensed this moment coming—not urgently, not insistently, but with the quiet certainty that something unfinished was finally ready to be set down. This presence felt different from Terry's earlier visits. There was no agitation now. No pressure.

She centered herself before speaking.

"I feel you, Terry. You can come in."

The air shifted, almost imperceptibly. She saw him first as a shimmer, then as something more defined, until Terry stood before her. He was recognizably himself, but the sharp edge that had once surrounded him was gone. What remained was calm—at ease and steady.

Sarah understood. This wasn't another visit. It was goodbye.

I knew I wasn't ready before, Terry said. *There was one more thing to do.*

She nodded, remaining silent. This wasn't a moment for questions.

To thank you. You listened to me. You didn't push. You let me speak when I was ready.

"You're welcome," she said quietly, though she sensed he hadn't needed the words.

You gave me a voice when I no longer had one.

The line settled between them, simple and complete. Sarah felt its truth without needing to respond.

I wasn't easy to live with, Terry continued. *I had a sharp tongue. I refused to back down even when it would have cost me nothing to bend. And I took too much of that out on Donald.*

Sarah listened, her hand still resting on Max's back, the steady warmth anchoring her.

I'm not excusing what he did. That choice was his. But I can admit that I helped shape the resentment that grew between us. I see that now.

She met his gaze and inclined her head slightly. Understanding didn't require agreement.

There was a pause, then Terry spoke again, his tone quieter.

Gregor didn't deserve to be pulled into it. My anger over those trees went further than it should have. When it mattered, he showed up. He tried to help. That counts for something.

"That's true, but now there's also the opportunity for that to change," Sarah said.

I hope so. Small towns can be quick to judge and slow to admit they're wrong. But sometimes they get there.

As he spoke, Sarah noticed that his presence no longer held

the same weight. The edges of him seemed softer, less fixed, as though he no longer needed to remain.

Well, that's why I came. Thank you. I'm ready now.

She felt no fear from him. No hesitation. Just acceptance.

"I wish you peace, Terry," she said. "Goodbye."

He inclined his head in acknowledgement. Then his presence thinned, softened, and was simply gone.

Sarah remained where she was, the quiet settling around her. Max shifted and sighed, his breathing slow and even beneath her hand. The house felt the same as it always had—and yet different, as though something long held had finally been released.

A tear slipped down her cheek. It wasn't grief that brought it, but the impact of witnessing something finished.

She wiped it away and sat for another moment, letting the stillness do its work.

"Well, Max," she said at last, "that's that."

He licked her hand and returned to his bed.

Sarah turned back to her computer screen, took a deep breath and placed her hands on the keyboard, and let out a slow breath. Work waited. Life moved forward.

And that felt right.

CHAPTER THIRTY-FIVE

The ladies had finished their potluck dinner and cleaned the kitchen before retiring to the living room. There were still no quilt-of-the-month designs picked or projects started, which was rare for the group. They all felt that the time to move on hadn't arrived before, but tonight it had.

Kitchen chores done, they gathered together in comfy chairs, mugs of their favorite hot beverage in hand. Reuben even decided to join them and was curled up beside Eva on the couch, just like he did when Jim was there.

"Have you ever noticed how quiet it feels after a case has been solved?" Eva asked.

"I hadn't really thought about it before, but you're right. It's like we need a brief respite before the action begins again," Jennifer replied.

"Please don't use the word 'action.' It makes it sound too much like that's what's waiting for us," Sarah said, but her usual levity wasn't softening the sentiment. She was still processing her last contact with Terry.

"Good point," Annalise agreed. "It's almost like we expect it to be part of the club's routine."

And you're surprised by that? Isn't that what happens every month? Reuben asked, his snark creeping in.

Eva translated for him.

"It's not that we *expect* it to happen, Reuben," Annalise replied, then paused. "But it does seem to happen more often than just coincidence. I've said it before—I think we were brought together for more than just friendship."

"I'd be happy to keep the friendship and let the other stuff go," Sarah said. She was still processing her visit from Terry and the thought of repeating the experience wasn't sparking joy.

"I'm still trying to understand how resentment between family members can turn into something so dangerous," Eva said. "Maybe it's just that I can't imagine that ever happening with my brother."

"It's probably been like that since the first humans. You would think we'd have evolved more by now, though," Annalise commented.

"I'm just glad Matt and Nicky get along so well. I think they'd do anything for each other—well, within reason," Jennifer amended.

That lightened the mood a little.

"There were so many facets of human behavior with this case," Annalise said. "And so many people affected in ways that shouldn't have happened. I'm most sad about Gregor."

"I saw him at the grocery store the other day, and it seemed like people who know him were going out of their way to be friendly," Eva commented. "He seems to be taking it in stride, but there's still an air of reserve about him. It's like he isn't ready to be vulnerable again."

"Can't say that I blame him," Jennifer agreed.

There was a loud thump as Reuben landed on the floor. He'd misjudged his proximity to the edge of the couch when he rolled over. As soon as he landed, he jumped to his feet and trotted to the bay window and his cushion. Everyone knew he was pretending to have done it on purpose, but held their remarks to preserve his dignity.

"I think that was a signal to change the topic," Eva remarked. "How did Matt like the quilt pattern you picked out, Jennifer? Or is it going to be a surprise?"

"I'm saving it as a surprise, but I think he'll like it. It will be a nice reminder of home instead of some generic store-bought bedspread."

"How are you holding up about it?" Annalise asked.

"There's so much going on to get ready for graduation, I haven't had time to dwell on it. That will kick in later. I'm hoping a new quilt project for the club will take my mind off it, too. So, anyone have any ideas?"

"It just so happens, I do. Janet Grainger from the Glen Lake Historical Society called me. They're looking for donations for an exhibit they're planning," Eva replied.

"Really? I hadn't heard about that," Annalise said, surprised.

"They had approached the senior center asking if anyone had quilts made by residents that were at least a hundred years old. They're planning a bicentennial celebration and are asking volunteers to make a modern interpretation of the quilt designs."

"That sounds like fun," Jennifer said.

"I might need some help with this project. I'm still not into the design stage of quilt making," Sarah said, her voice tentative.

"We're happy to help," Eva told her. "Depending on the original designs, it might even be possible to find a modern design someone has already made."

"As long as we don't need to make it in a month, I can fit it in. It would be a good challenge for me to make something bigger than a mug rug," Sarah said, her voice deprecating.

"Then are we in agreement?" Eva asked.

The others chimed in with their assent.

"In that case, the meeting is adjourned. I'll let you know what Janet has for us."

Everyone carried their mugs to the kitchen and said their goodbyes. After they'd left, Eva reflected on the project. *Something old asking to be understood again.*

As she settled into her senior years, sometimes that's how she felt, too.

She heard Reuben's soft snores beside her. He'd returned to the couch once everyone left and he no longer thought he might be at risk of humiliating himself.

"We all need to be understood, don't we?" she said softly, and stroked her hand down his back.

He stretched and opened one eye to look at her as if to let her know he agreed, and then went back to sleep. That was all that needed to be said.

~

Continue the Series
The story isn't over yet.
Return to Glen Lake and see what the quilt club uncovers next.
Explore the Cozy Quilts Club Mysteries

~

Stay Connected
Join my reader newsletter
Be the first to hear about new releases, special discounts, and exclusive bonus content.
Sign up for the Newsletter at marshadefilippo.com
OR
Get notified automatically when new books release.
Follow me on Amazon
Follow me on BookBub

~

A Quick Favor

Reviews help other readers discover the Cozy Quilts Club mysteries.

If you enjoyed this book, would you consider leaving a short review on Amazon? Even a few sentences make a difference.

Thank you for being part of the quilt circle.

ALSO BY MARSHA DEFILIPPO

Arizona Dreams (The Arizona Series)

Later-in-life romances about second chances, lasting love, and deep emotional connection—with on-page intimacy.

Arizona Dreams (Seasons of the Heart)

Later-in-life romances about second chances and lasting love—told in a clean, closed-door style.

The Destiny Inn series

A gentle magical-realism series set in a timeless inn, where travelers arrive when they need it most and leave forever changed.

A Cozy Quilts Club Mystery series

A cozy mystery series featuring a small-town quilt club whose members use their paranormal gifts to solve murders—one stitch at a time.

The Quilt of Forgotten Secrets

A Cozy Quilts Club Bonus Story. Available as Ebook and Audiobook formats

Read: https://BookHip.com/MCXWBJK

Listen: https://ihave.spoken.press/p/6f6i3VshmzU

ABOUT THE AUTHOR

After retiring from her day job of nearly 33 years, Marsha DeFilippo has embarked on a new career of writing books. She is also a quilter and lifelong avid crafter who has yet to try a craft she doesn't like. She spends her winters in Arizona and the remainder of the year in Maine.

**For more information, please visit my website:
marsha defilippo.com**

To get the latest information on new releases, excerpts and more, be sure to sign up for my newsletter.
https://marshadefilippo.com/newsletter

Follow me on Amazon
Click the **+Follow** button on my Amazon Author Page and Amazon will notify you when new books release.

facebook.com/Marsha-DeFilippo
instagram.com/marshadefilippo
bookbub.com/authors/marsha-defilippo
pinterest.com/defilippo0699
amazon.com/author/marshadefilippo
marshadefilippowriter.substack.com

www.ingramcontent.com/pod-product-compliance
Lightning Source LLC
Chambersburg PA
CBHW030930060726
47591CB00005B/1737